KAYLEIGH'S KNIGHT

COLLEEN MARIE

Copyright ©2025 by Colleen Marie Berry

Cover Copyright © 2025 by *Roseanna White Designs*

Interior formatting by *Hannah Linder Designs* First Edition

No part of this book may be reproduced or transmitted in any form or by any means, electronic or mechanical, including photocopying, recording, or by an information storage and retrieval system-except by a reviewer who may quote brief passages in a review to be printed in a magazine, newspaper, or on the Web-without permission in writing from the author.

All characters in this work are purely fictional and have no existence outside the imagination of the author and have no relation whatsoever to anyone bearing the same name or names. They are not even distantly inspired by any individual known or unknown to the author, and all incidents are pure invention.

ISBN: 979-8-218-58883-0

Published by Colleen Marie

www.onespiritoflove.com

To Jesus, my Knight and Savior

PROLOGUE

"We need more emotion. These are lines of love, so speak from the heart! Okay, please have a seat." Mrs. Bello waved her hand dismissively, and Ellie and Travis hurried to their seats. I looked back to the *Foundations of British Literature* script on my desk.

"We need two more people," Mrs. Bello murmured. She adjusted her red-framed glasses and glanced around the small classroom, pausing momentarily on a portrait of Jane Austen hanging on the wall.

She let out an audible sigh before catching my eye. "Oh, that will work nicely indeed!" After a moment of consideration her thin lips pulled into a grin. "Kayleigh, you will be Marianne."

Marianne, the middle Dashwood sister from Jane Austen's classic *Sense and Sensibility*. I tried to keep my face neutral, but inside I was thrilled. Marianne was my literary twin—the character I felt united with throughout the novel. I understood her romantic and passionate heart in more ways than one.

"And Chris, you will be our Mr. Willoughby!" Mrs. Bello

clapped her hands twice, the bangle bracelets chiming with her excitement. Her obvious satisfaction with her chosen characters evident in her upbeat stance.

While the rest of the class seemed to relax into their seats, safe from being called upon, heat prickled my cheeks. Chris Winters, the football quarterback, had never looked at me, let alone said anything to me. This past year I'd watched him from afar, dreaming of what it would be like to talk to him or have him smile at me in that way that made my heart skip. It looked like that was all about to change.

I pushed my dark, loose curls over my shoulder and walked to the front of the classroom, my fair skin pink with anticipation. The script crumpled in my tightening grip, and I forced my hand to relax.

"Alright, let's begin with—"

The bell rang before Mrs. Bello could finish. A mix of relief and disappointment washed over me. Chris watched me closely. His left dimple deepened as a smile grew. His brown eyes locked with mine, and I quickly averted my gaze and walked towards the door.

"Excuse me, Mrs. Bello?" His voice stopped me in my tracks. "Would it be possible for me and Kayleigh to read our lines next class?"

My mouth fell open in surprise at his question. *Chris Winters wants to read lines with me?*

"Why, of course! That would be delightful!" Mrs. Bello beamed at him. "It's good to see the young appreciate the fine work of Ms. Austen." She shot another glance at the portrait on the wall. "I look forward to seeing your embodiments of Marianne and Willoughby!"

She walked back to her desk and jotted a note on her large, flowery desk calendar before opening an old dictionary and flipping through the pages.

I adjusted my backpack and stared at him, too shocked to say or do anything more.

"I hope that's okay with you." Chris' head tilted slightly to the side, and amusement glinted in his eyes.

"It would be lovely."

It would be lovely? Apparently, I'm living in the Regency Era like Austen.

"Lovely," he echoed back. "See you tomorrow, Kayleigh."

Then he walked out the door, right past Maddie, who was waiting patiently for me. She rolled her eyes, and I followed her into the hallway. As I fell into step next to my closest friend since grade school, I felt like I was in a dream.

"I'm in love." I sighed—a big, dramatic one that would make even Mrs. Bello proud. "We're going to be Marianne and Willoughby."

Maddie adjusted her tortoiseshell circular rimmed glasses. "You do know that Marianne doesn't actually end up with Willoughby though, right?"

Of course I knew that, but it wasn't the time to get technical. Love wasn't something to put perimeters on. Love was a matter of the heart, just like Mrs. Bello said.

Maddie nudged me with her elbow. "I didn't think Chris Winters was your type."

"Isn't he everyone's type?"

She scrunched her nose. "No. Not at all."

"You're just not a romantic like me."

"True. You do take it to a whole new level. Just remember, not everything is like a novel."

I linked my arm through hers and pushed the comment from my mind. "Come on. Let's get to algebra."

As we passed Chris and his friends standing by the lockers, he sent me a look that promised this was only the beginning.

CHAPTER ONE

"I can't believe you're breaking up with me."

Chris runs a hand through his thick, light brown hair and sends a desperate look towards the door of the coffee shop. "Kayleigh, listen, we've been over this. You're going to Ireland, and I'm off to 'Bama. Promised first backup to the quarterback." He speaks like this should be explanation enough.

It's always about football. I mean, it's not like he's even starting on the team. The first-string quarterback literally has to get injured for him to even play. And what's with all the 'Bama talk recently? I guess it's too hard to say the full name of the state. *Al-a-ba-ma.* Nope. Not hard at all.

"But," I say, trying to focus, "I thought our relationship was—*is*—more important than that. Didn't we say our love was unbreakable?"

He clenches his jaw. "No, you said that."

"And you agreed! You said we could make it work. That we would find a way. That love conquers all!" A few heads turn our way as my voice rises. I cringe inwardly at my pleading tone and use of awkward clichés.

Chris shoots another longing look towards the door. *Did he ever look at me like that?* I push the question from my mind.

"Again, that was you." His voice is slow and pointed, emphasizing the last word in a heartbreaking punch.

Could I really have gotten this so wrong?

"But," I whisper in a shaky voice, "I love you."

He takes a deep breath and slowly exhales before reaching across the table for my hand. "This is for the best. Our lives are going in two different directions. We need to see what's out there, you know?"

A runaway tear slides down the curve of my cheek, and I fight the urge to wipe it away.

"Alright." Chris stands in a definitive movement. He drops a few bills on the table, covering the yellow shabby chic style linen napkins like a storm cloud covering the shining sun. "You'll see this is for the best. Good luck, Kayleigh." With a dismissive nod he walks out the door, bell chiming like the turning of a page in one of my audiobooks. The sound of a chapter ending.

Good Luck? After two-and-a-half-years together, that's my goodbye?

"Can I get you anything else?" Jamie asks tentatively. Jamie, the unlucky server assigned to our table, is a sophomore on the Forest Haven school newspaper. As her editor for the past two years, I've had the chance to see her grow as a reporter and served as a mentor to her, showing her the ropes of the journalism club.

She stares at me now with a mixture of pity and what could only be described as excitement gleaming in her eyes. Like a cat that finally caught the mouse. Apparently, I was louder than I realized, and this story is just too good to pass up. The savageness of journalism strikes me, and not for the first time. There's little room left for humanity when the story is there, ready for the taking.

"Ah, no thank you, Jamie." I put on my best *everything is just perfect* smile, one that I've perfected over the years. I hand her the check and money, with only a slight tremble in my hands.

I walk out the cafe door with my head held high. I manage to trip only once before making my way onto Main Street—a feat if there ever was one in my current emotional state. The sun is setting on the familiar sight of the small-town shops and cafes. I take a deep breath to calm my nerves before the short walk home.

Head high, shoulders back. And just keep walking.

Magnolia catches me as I turn the corner. "Oh, Kayleigh." She wraps me in a big bear hug. "Don't worry. You'll find your knight in shining armor one day. And when you do, you'll ride off into the sunset together."

My last vestige of control threatens to break.

"I'm fine, Magnolia, really. But, I've gotta go." My voice cracks and the tears burn, screaming for an escape. I nearly run down the street.

A backward glance reveals Magnolia's heart-shaped face is lined with concern. She has been a true friend to me over the past couple years. Her shoulder-length blonde hair is tied up in a loose bun on the top of her head. A few stray strands have come loose and hang around her peaches and cream complexion. When Magnolia bought the run-down cafe, she transformed it into the coziest alcove in downtown Berryville, Maryland. At just eighteen, she won the county's entrepreneur of the year award when Magnolia's Cafe opened four years ago. I was beginning my freshman year at Forest Haven, and the cafe was a place that immediately felt like a second home.

I've always thought that Magnolia ended up in Berryville for a reason. Her parents owned their own restaurant and tearoom, specializing in British cuisine and glamorous tea service, in her hometown of Boston. Magnolia was home-schooled and earned her high school diploma a year-and-a-half early, allowing her to take business classes at a local university. She worked closely with her parents in their business and looked forward to running the business on her own one day. That day came sooner than she expected.

One rainy night, Magnolia's parents were killed in a car accident by a drunk driver, leaving Magnolia, their only child, brokenhearted and alone. It was too hard to continue on alone in the restaurant and their family's brownstone, so she sold the business and family home. She packed her car with all her worldly possessions, including her mother's collection of tea sets, and began driving south. Her course eventually took her through Berryville. She stopped in front of the run-down, boarded-up, white-shingled cafe with a For Sale sign, and knew it was meant for her. It was the literal sign she was looking for. Within a few days, the cafe was hers, and both she and the cafe had a new chance at life.

I've spent so much time in Magnolia's Cafe that I can easily fill in on days when she needs help. But most days, I sit at the small back corner table, that has unofficially become my table. I open my notebook and lay it next to the glass vase with a single rose that Magnolia keeps fresh on all of the tables. My lined notebook pages are filled with pencil scribbled story ideas and poems. People strolling by the window become the inspiration for characters in my stories.

Magnolia is the one whom I share my stories with. We can talk for hours about the drama of high school, which Magnolia says is nothing compared to the spectacle of adulthood. We dream together about our fairytale endings over hot tea or slices of warm cherry pie topped with homemade vanilla ice cream from Bluebell Creamery. Magnolia dreams that the love of her life will walk through the door of the cafe one day, sweep her off her feet, and the rest will be history. She's a romantic like me. Or like I used to be—before Chris broke my heart right there in the cafe full of dreams.

My breathing becomes more rapid as I turn down the lane to our farm. The sight of our 1800s-style white farmhouse is like the sun peeking out among the stormy clouds. Claddagh Farm and Animal Rescue hangs from the curved pinewood arch, its boldly carved letters sending a message that this land is a refuge for the unwanted and downtrodden. It's a place of new beginnings. What began as a run-down farmhouse and overgrown land is now one of the most endearing and inspiring farms in Maryland.

Instead of going into the house, I walk past the horse pasture, ignoring the whinnies of the horses by the fence. I fix my eyes on the duck pond—my little corner of the farm. When I was younger, I begged Dad to build a pond, and for my ninth birthday him and Mom surprised me with the most magnificent 250-square-foot pond filled with fish, lily pads, and a running waterfall. Over the years, a fully sustainable ecosystem developed. Dragonflies, beetles, and mayflies colonized shortly after the fish were established. Frogs, toads, salamanders, turtles, and snails followed, creating a balance in my little corner of the farm.

At the sight of the rippling water and floating lily pads, my heart regains its steady rhythm. I sit on the black metal bench and run my fingers over the soft flowing branch of the neighboring willow tree. The tree roots are deep and resilient, while the branches are delicate and graceful—a perfect combination of strength and vulnerability. Few things bring me more peace than watching the water flow over the large stones of the arching waterfall.

A paw prods my leg, and I look down at Marianne, my blue merle Australian shepherd. I stroke her fur and wonder if her name was such a good idea after all. I was blinded by the idea of first love and a dream that had little resemblance to reality.

I hold her chin and whisper, "Why is this happening, girl?"

She stares back at me with concern in her stunning combination of blue, brown, and gold flecked eyes. Tilting her head to the side, she looks at me like I have all of the answers in the world. In reality, I don't have any answers.

At the sound of quacking, she jumps up and begins herding the ducklings behind their mother.

"Eleanor, you're a good mother." I coo to the large white American Pekin duck as she waddles to the pond. Pekins are usually raised for meat, but Eleanor just showed up at our small pond one day and never left. When Dad mentioned keeping her for a roast, I broke into tears swearing I would care for her, and she deserved a second chance like the other animals on our farm.

Dad relented and now Eleanor has a brood of six ducklings.

"Marianne, no!" I scold as she nips at the last duckling before he hops into the water.

Marianne's apologetic eyes turn to me as she lowers her head.

"It's okay. Come here, girl."

I can't stay mad at her since she's just doing what she was bred to do. Australian shepherds are highly intelligent and have a strong herding instinct. They often nip at the heels of cows and sheep to keep them moving in the intended direction. Unfortunately, a duckling isn't as durable as the cattle and can get hurt a lot easier, so more care is needed.

When Mom came home with her, just an eight-week-old puppy with a broken right front leg, abandoned at their veterinary center, she looked like a matted ball of black, white, and grey tricolor fur. We don't know who dropped her off at the center, but my parents are basically famous out here as the dynamic duo of vets. They have a reputation for taking in those most in need without any question or inquiry. They are a safe haven in our community. And while their focus is on horses, they are known to care for small animals when needed. My parents founded O'Reilly Equine Veterinary over two decades ago, not only a highly respected practice in our small town of Berryville, but the whole state of Maryland.

I took over the duty of nursing Marianne back to health. When her leg mended and she was fit and healthy enough to explore the farm, I took her to meet my favorite duck in the world. Marianne and Eleanor were friends from the moment they saw each other. More like family than friends really, so I thought the names of two of the sisters from Jane Austen's *Sense and Sensibility* were appropriate for the two girls.

I have a bit of a Jane Austen obsession, and *Sense and Sensibility* is my favorite of her novels. Reading her stories sophomore year changed my view of the whole literary world. Always an avid reader, I took to writing and now spend every free moment doing one or the other. And when I can't read or write, I'm dreaming up stories.

A gargled honking sounds as Juliet, our female swan, reminds Eleanor's ducklings to keep their distance from her path. As the ducklings swim closer to the protective wings of their mother, Juliet sends a satisfied look to her mate, Romeo. Watching them together is seeing love in action. Most swans bond with a mate for life. When one passes away, the other will grieve, just like we do. Romeo and Juliet have been together for the better part of five years now.

Second chances are big in our family. Never one to throw away something because it's broken, we take that same philosophy with the animals. My older sister Teagan and her boyfriend and science research partner Finn started an equine-assisted therapy program in Cloverdale, Ireland where they attend Emerald Isle University—the same university I will be at this time tomorrow.

Being at the pond has done the trick again, and I'm feeling more at ease than I could have imagined an hour ago. Rounding the back of the house, I stop in my tracks.

How could I have forgotten about my going-away party?

It's like a punch in the gut to see the couples dancing under the twinkling lights of the gazebo. Silver and gold streamers sway in the breeze as a soft piano melody drifts through the air, creating a magical dreamlike atmosphere.

My stomach turns at the thought of having to face everyone. The vision I once had of dancing with Chris floats away on the light breeze, replaced with an intense loneliness.

"There you are!" Teagan's voice breaks through my thoughts as she wraps me in a big sister hug.

Teagan is the oldest at nineteen. Often mistaken for twins, we have the same long dark hair and sky blue eyes. At five foot six, we're a good four inches taller than our youngest sister, Ashling. And while we all have the same fair complexion, Ashling's is scattered with freckles; her auburn hair and bright green eyes set her apart.

Ashling tilts her head and studies me. "Are you okay?"

"Of course," I reply, a little too quickly.

She raises an eyebrow. "Really? Because you look like how I feel at these parties."

Even in my mood, I can't help the small laugh that escapes my lips. "Yeah, well, it's not exactly how I dreamed this particular party would be."

Teagan glances around. "If you don't like the decorations, we could—"

"No, it's not the decorations. Everything is perfect." I wave a hand around the yard. "It's just...Chris broke up with me."

While they look surprised at this announcement, neither

look particular unhappy about it. They exchange a not-too-subtle look, and I clear my throat expectantly.

"I'm so sorry, Kay," Teagan finally says, taking my hand. "That's...awful." Something in her tone doesn't ring quite true.

Ashling fails to stop the grin forming on her lips.

"Why are you smiling?" I narrow my eyes at her.

Teagan glances back and forth between us, worry evident in her expression. Ashling and I have a long history of not seeing eye to eye—something she never seems to hide.

Ashling considers my question before unabashedly allowing her smile to grow. "Because I'm glad you guys broke up."

Heat creeps up my neck, prickling my cheeks.

Teagan holds up a hand. "I'm sure Ashling means—"

"I mean what I said. And she knows what I mean." Ashling looks me straight in the eyes. "I'm sorry you're upset right now, but honestly you deserve so much more than him and that relationship."

Tears burn my eyes, and Ashling's expression falters. "Kayleigh, you're my sister and I love you. So much. But, I'm not going to lie to you. And I think in time you will agree that this is a good thing."

I bite my bottom lip to keep it from shaking.

"He's a jerk, Kay. He always has been."

I feel the urge to defend him, but I can't find the words. I tell myself this is because I'm not feeling like myself at the moment and not because there's any truth in her words.

"Listen." Ashling takes my other hand. "Just say the word, and I'll head over there right now and give him a piece of my mind."

I let out a pained laugh and wipe the few runaway tears.

"I love you both," I tell them.

That's the thing with my sisters—no matter what happens I know we will always be there for each other.

———

It may be a party in my honor, but I'm drifting about the grounds without actually connecting with anyone. I slide through the side gate and round the corner of the house. I stop just out of sight and lean against the old maple tree. As I close my eyes, images from the cafe flash before me.

He's gone.

Everything I imagined about the future included him. After college, Chris would take over his family's banking business while I would accept an offer for a prestigious reporter position. We would get married in our town chapel and have a huge ball as our reception. Then, when we started a family, I would stay home with our babies while working part-time for the newspaper. It would be perfect.

A perfect disaster. The thought comes before I can stop it. Did I always somehow know it was going to turn out this way?

"Hi."

The soft scent of lemon wafts through the air.

"I'm sorry I left like that," I whisper to Magnolia as I open my eyes and see her standing by me.

"Oh, Kayleigh, my heart breaks for you." She gives me one of her warm smiles that lets you know she genially cares. "You know I'm always here. And I'll be in Ireland in just a couple of months." She leans against the tree next to me.

Magnolia is always there for me. She been saying that she's due for a vacation, but she hasn't had one since opening the cafe. This is the perfect time for a trip to Ireland. A break for her and a much-needed comfort to me. And I'm even more grateful for her upcoming visit now.

Excitement and dread fight for dominance in my heart. "Thanks. I'm just...trying to figure this all out. It was so unexpected."

She averts her eyes, much like Teagan and Ashling had done. Does everyone have a secret dislike of our relationship that I never knew about? And as it seems to be the case, why didn't anyone say anything?

"I wish he hadn't left so quickly." Magnolia walks a few steps towards the rose bushes before turning back around. "I would have loved to have thrown him out of the cafe."

"I would've liked seeing that." That's an image I can appreciate right now.

"You and me both."

"How has my life changed so much in just a few hours?" It's like I turned the page in one of my books, and it's blank.

"On a positive note, you have a chance for a fresh start in Ireland. You never know what—or who—you will meet. It may actually be perfect timing." She says this with more excitement than I feel.

But the thought does lift my spirit ever so slightly. "When God closes a door, He opens a window, right?"

"Absolutely. And maybe this window will give you a chance to find yourself again. You were with Chris for so long that it was like your whole life was centered on him and your future with him."

How true her words are. "You're saying that I let everything revolve around him and what he wanted?"

She considers this. "Not exactly."

"But close enough?"

It's her turn to sigh. "When he was around, it was like you were only part of yourself."

I begin to protest, but I'm reminded of what Ashling said. Magnolia and my sisters know me better than anyone. Maybe they are right. And the fact that I'm not completely denying it says more than their words do.

Magnolia watches me for a moment before continuing. "Now you are completely free to be yourself all of the time. And I, for one, am so excited to see it."

I always tried to be the perfect girlfriend to Chris, but I never considered what I was losing in the process. I wasn't completely myself around him. In being his girlfriend, I lost a part of myself. I never thought about it before, but looking at it now, I see it in a new way. Even so, it still doesn't take away the hurt. But maybe this will be a much-needed fresh start.

"You're right," I say, determination edging my shaky voice. "Maybe Chris dumping me is a blessing after all."

The crack of my voice when I say his name causes the sympathy to deepen in Magnolia's eyes.

"Not maybe. Definitely," I say, stronger now. "I'm going to take a page from Elizabeth Bennett's book."

The sympathy fades to pride. "A good heroine if there ever was one."

I nod. "She never let anyone walk over her or push her aside."

"No, she didn't," Magnolia agrees. "But, remember the whole pride and prejudice thing. Don't let what happened with Chris make you assume all guys are like him."

"True." I recall the love story of Elizabeth Bennett and Mr. Darcy. How mistaken they were at the beginning because of their preconceived notions.

"But, if you run into a Mr. Collins, stay as far away as you can."

We both giggle at her reference to the pompous, conceited, and materialistic clergyman vowing to win Elizabeth's hand in marriage. It's become a thing with me and Magnolia to warn each other of the Mr. Collins of the world. The weight on my chest lifts just the slightest bit, but before

I can enjoy the feeling, a shrill shriek stops our laughter. Glancing behind us, I spot Tori Banks balancing on one leg as she removes her white sandal, covered in dog mess. Her long blonde hair falls over her shoulder as she shows the two immaculately dressed girls with her the soiled shoe.

I groan. "Why did she of all people have to step in it?"

Magnolia grimaces. "Well, it is a farm. You need to watch where you're walking. Everyone knows that."

"Tori has never been one for this or any farm." I watch as she waves her hand in front of her nose.

"Honestly, how you two are even friends amazes me." She shakes her head.

Tori holds the hands of the two girls on either side of her and hops to the wooded bench. Once she's seated on the bench, Alice Dean, the shorter of the two girls, takes the sandal and hurries away—no doubt ready to clean it herself. Jackie Horn, the taller girl, sits by Tori, comforting her with wide-eyed panic like this is the worst thing that could possibly happen.

"We're not really friends." As soon as the words are out of my mouth, it is both a sad and freeing admission. Tori and I only started hanging out after Chris and I began dating. She was the captain of the dance team and dating Luke Jones, Chris' best friend and the tight end on the football team. My stomach sinks at the realization that I will have to tell people we broke up.

"Now that one, I've always liked." Magnolia points to a short girl in white jeans and a yellow and white checkered buttoned-down shirt with the sleeves rolled up to her elbows. Maddie's wearing brown cowgirl boots—ones that are worn in and aged from her time competing in barrel racing. Her shoulder-length, wavy, sandy blonde hair is pulled into a high ponytail revealing a round, freckled complexion and light brown eyes behind brown and tan glasses. Long white feathers swing from her ears as she throws a ball for Marianne, who catches it midleap by the gazebo. Her bobbed tail wags with excitement as she bounds back to Maddie.

"Kayleigh!" Tori's high-pitched voice calls from the bench. She slips her now clean sandal back on her foot and hurries over to us, Alice and Jackie at her heels. "I'm so sorry to hear about you and Chris. I just can't believe it. I bet he will come to his senses and come crawling back."

I guess I won't have to tell people after all.

"Maybe she doesn't want him crawling back at all." Magnolia's soft voice is a contradiction to Tori's overly loud tone.

Tori raises an eyebrow at Magnolia like no one in their right mind would ever not want Chris. Magnolia stares right back at her.

Would I want Chris back? Part of me jumps at the thought of us getting back together and everything being the back to how it was. But the other part, the newer part, wants to keep that door closed.

"Hi, Tori," I finally say, my voice steadier than I feel. "It was a surprise, but I think it will all work out for the best."

"Well," she says, obvious disappointment in her expression, "I hope it will. And I'll be at 'Bama with Chris, so I'll be sure to put in a good word."

My hands tighten into fists.

"I don't think there's any need for that," Magnolia says, throwing a protected glance my way.

Tori is about to reply, but I cut her off. "Looks like the food's ready." I point toward the backyard tables and my escape from this conversation.

I guide Tori and the girls over to the food table and then step to the side with Magnolia and Maddie.

"You okay?" Maddie takes a bite of her brisket sandwich.

I sigh. "Marianne doesn't end up with Willoughby. Just

like I don't end up with Chris. That day in Brit Lit seems like a lifetime ago, and only yesterday at the same time. I thought we were destined to be together. I was just as naive and ridiculous as Marianne had been. I guess I should expect a deadly fever soon, one where I can sort through the mess of my life and come out on the other side with renewed hope and understanding."

"Or," Maddie says, "maybe you can avoid the serendipitous walk in the cold rain and near-death experience and just go straight to the reevaluation of your life part."

"Now, that is a plan," Magnolia says. "And remember, if Marianne hadn't lost Willoughby, she would never have found her true love in Colonel Brandon."

Maddie nods. "And theirs was a love that lasts. You just have to be open to a new adventure."

A new adventure feels right in this moment. In a few hours I leave for Ireland, the land of saints and scholars, and nothing is holding me back. I have the distinct feeling that what's about to come around the corner will forever change my life

CHAPTER TWO

I arrive at the Dublin airport just before two in the afternoon the next day. I get through customs quickly and find myself outside by the car park thirty minutes early. I look to the cloudless sky as the sunshine warms my face. But, even the brightness of the day doesn't drive away the residual gloom and exhaustion of the past twenty-four hours.

"I thought it was supposed to be rainy in Ireland," I murmur to myself.

"Ah, there's a fifty-fifty chance any day."

I turn toward the masculine voice with the deep Irish lilt. A man stands in what appears to be full medieval knight regalia.

"I didn't realize I went back in time, as well as across the Atlantic." I block the sun with my hand and catch a handsome and familiar face smiling back at me.

"I am a grand Knight of Kerry, m' lady." He takes my hand and kisses the top.

Warm tingles spread across my skin at the touch of his lips, and I pull my hand away.

There's a questioning gleam in his hazel eyes. "Kayleigh. How are ya doin'?"

"Seamus Murphy." His name rolls off my tongue, sounding like the name of a hero from a long-ago legend.

He grins back at me from the chain mail framing his chiseled face. We met last summer when my family visited Teagan at the end of her first year at Emerald Isle University. He's the nephew of the Kavanaghs, the family that housed Teagan and Finn during their summer science research program, and a bar tender at O'Callahan's, a popular pub in Dublin, close to the university.

"Good to see you," I say, a bit breathy.

"Heard ya would be here this year. Bet ya're lookin' forward to it, right?"

Am I looking forward to this year?

"Sure," I say, not knowing if it's an honest answer or not.

He seems to sense my indecision and is about to say something but nods behind me instead. "Looks like yer ride's here."

I turn around and see Teagan and Finn walking towards us. Teagan took an earlier flight last night to meet up with Finn this morning. Seeing her here makes the events of yesterday come back to life. I catch Seamus watching me closely.

"What?"

Before he can answer, Teagan and Finn join us.

"I'm so glad you're here!" Teagan wraps me in a hug.

"I can't really believe that I'm here. It feels a bit surreal."

"Enjoy every minute of this," Teagan says. "Look at this beautiful day—it has to be a sign."

She pulls back, and looks up into the blue cloudless sky.

"Teagan told me about Chris. I'm so sorry, Kayleigh." Finn gives me a side hug. "Teagan's right, though. There's something magical about Ireland."

The two of them look longingly into each other's eyes, and I avert my gaze.

Seamus clears his throat. "Bad luck with yer fella?"

The humiliation comes back. "You could say that."

When no one says anything, I continue. "It was a stupid idea anyway."

"What was a stupid idea?" Finn asks, looking as confused as the other two.

I give a shaky laugh. "True love."

They stare at me without saying anything. I guess it is a shocking statement coming from me, considering I've always been the romantic one. I was such a fool living in a fairytale. I reach for my suitcases, but Seamus gets them first.

"Where are ye parked?" He asks Teagan and Finn.

"Right over there." Finn points to the pickup truck to the right.

As we walk to the truck, I watch Seamus carrying my bags and, for a reason I don't understand, it annoys me. "I guess chivalry isn't dead after all. Although you are just pretending to be a knight, right?" I force the playful tone, but there's a bite to my words.

He shoots me a look that sends a flash of those unexpected tingles through me. "With the right fella, it wouldn't be a question."

"So, Seamus," Teagan says, "are you heading over to the festival from here?"

It's a clear change of the subject, and I realize that I have absolutely no idea why he's dressed like a knight and at the airport in the first place.

"Aye. As soon as Eoin gets here."

We reach the truck, and Seamus puts my bags in the back tailgate and hooks them to the side with a pulley.

"Eoin is Seamus' friend from secondary school," Finn explains. "They played rugby together growing up. He's in

Canada now, interning as a sports reporter. Seamus said he wouldn't miss the festival though. It's a big tradition around here."

"What festival?"

Teagan puts her hand over her mouth. "Oh, Kay, I thought I told you. There's a big Medieval Festival in Cloverdale every year. Seamus is the Knight of Kerry this year."

"That right." Seamus beams, apparently over my recent jab. "It's my year. I've been waitin' for this since I was a lad." His ruggedly handsome face takes on a boyish glow with these words. "I'll see ya there?"

"We wouldn't miss it, man." Finn opens the passenger door for Teagan.

"Will ya be there too?" Seamus asks me.

I do love time period festivals. The medieval period was filled with tales of adventure, forgiveness, and courtly love. Knights went to all extremes to win the lady who captured his heart. They didn't tire of their love or push it to the side for better things. It was a love to die for. How many people could say they'd die for their love today? Certainly not Chris.

"No, I don't think so." I climb into the truck. "But, have fun pretending to be a knight."

"Who says I'm pretending?" And with that, he turns, armor glinting in the sun, and walks back to the airport looking very much like a true knight.

TEN MINUTES into the twenty-minute drive to the university, Finn slows the car to a halt.

"I've heard that there's often sheep traffic jams in Ireland, but you never told me people fill the roads too." I wind the window down and watch as three men stand in the middle of the road, deep in conversation and oblivious to us waiting. One of them is telling a story as he waves his arms around, causing another round of laughter from his buddies. Their cars are blocking the road, and there's no way around them without riding in the soft ground on either side.

Teagan sighs. "Yeah. This was hard for me to get used to at first, but it happens all of the time, especially when the sun is out. And it looks like rain in a bit, so it's like a free for all now."

"The Irish never miss an opportunity to talk with a neighbor," Finn agrees. "And schedules are a lot more lenient around here. When someone tells the time, we've learned it is really more of a loose estimate."

I laugh at this because it's the complete opposite of my schedule-following sister. "Teagan, how do you feel about that?"

She grimaces. "I'll admit, it took some getting used to. And some days, it can still send me into a bit of a panic, but I'm learning to enjoy the slower pace and connection."

They smile at each other, their love so evident. They didn't have an easy path finding love. Teagan fell for Finn when they were chemistry lab partners sophomore year in high school. He was the mysterious new boy in school, and she was dating someone. But, as they worked together, they quietly fell in love. Nothing was ever said, but the connection was strong. Then, one day during junior year, Finn left when his dad was transferred for his job. Teagan thought she would never see Finn again, but the summer after graduation they found themselves partnered in the Emerald Isle Science Research Internship. During their time working together at Brigid's Crossing, the Kavanagh's horse farm, their past feelings reignited, and they finally shared their true feelings for each other. They have been together ever since, and now, in their sophomore year at the university, they are as close as ever. Their love is a true love.

Well, if true love even exists.

"How's *Second Chances*?" I ask, looking for a distraction to my thoughts.

Teagan shifts towards me. "Wonderful! The program is just taking off. We are working with Caitlin Doherty from Donegal Equine Therapy, and she is amazing. I can't wait for you to meet her."

Teagan has this light in her eyes whenever she speaks about equine-assisted therapy. She has followed in Mom and Dad's footsteps with her love for all things equine. Even as little kids, she was drawn to the horses while I leaned more towards the dogs and my little pond. There is something about the loyalty of a dog and the serenity of the water that touches my soul. Teagan found a way to unite her passions for horses and science research in their equine-assisted activities program. They named it *Second Chances* because their program gives people a second chance at life. It's what my parents have created with our farm at home, and Teagan has brought that to Brigid's Crossing. It feels like our family farm has a place in Ireland now too.

I can't help but wonder if I will ever have that same light in my eyes that Teagan has now that she's doing exactly what she is called to do. It's not just a job or a career but a vocation.

Finn waves to the three men as we are finally able to drive around them. "Caitlin's helped us to structure our program to allow for government funded sessions with people who could otherwise not take part in the program. And her knowledge of the history of equine-assisted therapy and horses in general is incredible."

"So true," Teagan agrees. "She has so much experience with horses, even though she's only in her mid-thirties. She knows about the history of horses in Ireland in a way that you can only discover living here and having generations of knowledge and experience passed down through her family and friends."

They both sound completely in awe of Caitlin Dougherty. "She sounds like a great partner for you guys. How did you meet her?"

"That's the funny part," Teagan says. "She called us after everything with the emerald last year. She said that Mr. Banwell, a representative from the science research board at Emerald Isle, contacted her about our research proposal."

"Yeah." Finn turns around the bend and waves to a farmer on the side of the road. "She just offered us a partnership right over the phone. Called it a mentorship, saying Mr. Banwell has big plans."

Teagan shrugs. "We're still not sure what his big plans are, but hooking us up with Caitlin has been huge for *Second Chances*."

When Emerald Isle University comes into view, dark clouds have descended, and the threat of rain seems imminent now—a distinct change from the earlier brightness.

Finn pulls onto the long stone drive to the residence hall. Teagan cranes her neck to get a view of the science wing to the side.

"So," Teagan says with a big smile, "are you ready?"

Am I ready? A part of me is, but the other part wants to climb into my bed and hide under the covers for the foreseeable future.

I don't respond but follow her gaze through the window. The historic stone glistens in the light drizzle. Each stone builds the foundation with strength and dignity. How many scholars have walked the stone paths and sat in the lecture halls debating with other great minds. How many writers sat on the benches contemplating the next word in their story or line of their poem? I am not struck with inspiration at the sight of the university, like I hoped I would be, but I do see how it could be inspiring.

Could that be enough to make Emerald Isle a home?

AFTER SAYING goodbye to Teagan and Finn, I make my way down the hallway to the student check-in table. Out the window, I see them walking hand in hand to the science research building, full of excitement. There's a similar energy coming from the students around me, but as much as I try, I'm not feeling it.

"Name?" A perky woman with fiery red, chin-length hair and a gold nose stud looks at me expectantly. Her gray eyes are heavily lined in black, and her deep purple lips are pursed as she waits for my response.

"Kayleigh." I shift my weight from one foot to the other.

She rolls her eyes. "Last name?"

"Oh." The word sounds as ridiculous as I feel. "O'Reilly."

She doesn't respond as she scans the list of names in front of her. "Room 120."

"Great. Thank you." I take a few steps to the right.

"Wait," she calls, exasperation obvious in her tone. "Yer key." She holds up a silver key attached to a yellow plastic tag with the room number written on it.

"Right." I take the key from her before continuing down the hallway.

"It's the other direction," she calls again.

Of course it is.

"Thanks," I mumble as I pass her and hurry down the other hallway. I hope my luck is about to change.

I FIND my room down the second corridor and insert the silver key into the lock. As I turn it to the right, the key stops abruptly. I try to twist it back in the other direction, but it won't budge.

I groan. "I need a break." I twist the key harder until a snap echoes in the hallway.

I stare at the broken key in the palm of my hand. "That's not the kind of break I meant," I say through gritted teeth.

What do I do now? I really don't want to go back to the check-in table. I look around, hoping the answer will be clear, when I spot a large sign for the university newspaper. "Sign-Up" is printed in large red letters on top of a printed black and white newspaper page. I make my way to the other end of the hallway and stop just outside the newspaper office. An old brown clipboard with a lined sheet of white paper hangs from a large pin on a bulletin board. A pencil is tied to a string and secured next to the clipboard with a blue thumbtack.

"Are you a reporter too?"

I turn to see a stunning girl with coiled soft black hair and creamy mahogany skin. Her face is makeup free but naturally vibrant. Her white sweater, blue jeans, and brown ankle boots give off a girl-next-door look.

"Yes." Why does the idea of being a reporter suddenly feel so foreign to me. "I was just about to sign up."

"Me too," she says with a genuine smile.

"Freshman?" I ask, hopeful. It would be nice to have a friend on campus.

"Yes, an official newbie trying to find my way around." She shakes her head as she looks around, wide-eyed.

"It's a lot," I agree. "I think it's going to take some getting used to."

"I'm with you on that." She extends a hand. "I'm Samara."

"Kayleigh." I shake her hand and try to gauge her accent. "Are you from the US too?"

"Born and raised in Siesta Key, Florida."

"Oh, we went there on vacation once when I was a kid!" I think back to the beautiful white sand beaches and crystal clear water of the Gulf of Mexico. "I remember when we went snorkeling, and I saw the most incredible sea turtle. I swam with it until my parents said it was time to go in."

She laughs. "The sea turtles are amazing. All of the marine animals are. I may be a journalism major but couldn't think of leaving the sea behind, so I'm doing a marine biology minor. The marine animals have always been such a big part of my life."

I think back to our farm. "I understand that. You must really miss it."

"I'm definitely missing the beach now with this weather. But hopefully things here will settle down and feel more like home soon." She gets a faraway look in her eyes, and I can tell she's a little unsure of her place here too, making me feel instantly connected to her. "So, where are you from?" she asks.

"I'm from a small town called Berryville in northern Maryland. I grew up on a horse farm and animal rescue. So while it wasn't the beach, I understand your love for animals. But, like you, the water has always drawn me. We spend a lot of time throughout the year on Assateague Island."

"I've always wanted to go there! They have the wild horses, right?"

"Yeah. My sister Teagan loved watching them when we were kids. Actually, she still does—she works with horses."

"That's awesome. I'd love to be a writer for National Geographic one day. Although I know that's a far-fetched idea."

"My dad always says that a far-fetched idea is how every good idea started."

"I like that." She jots the phrase down on a slip of paper and sticks it in her bag. "I will have to keep that one close."

We compare our schedules and realize we have the Saints and Scholars core writing class together. The course serves as an advisor and mentee time as well as a class.

We sign our names on the clipboard.

"I need to get back to my room and finish unpacking." Samara points down the right corridor.

"I just want to get into my room." I pull the broken key out of my pocket.

She looks at the metal fragment in my hand. "Bad luck, huh?"

"It seems that's all I'm having recently." The pressure on my chest is back, and I take a deep breath.

"Well, I bet that's all about to change. You *are* in Ireland now."

"That is true." I want to share in her opportunistic attitude, but all I can think of is how the Irish have had just as much bad luck as good in their history. But I know she is right in perspective. I *am* in Ireland. Not long ago this was just a dream. I may have had a string of bad luck, but it looks like I just made my first friend at the university. That's a good thing. And I've signed up for the newspaper. The prospect of writing for a university paper gives me a little needed boost. Once I start reporting again I will feel more like myself.

———

THANKS to the kind man in maintence, I finally get into my room. I see that one side of the small room is already taken. The white-painted walls must be designed to make the room appear larger, which it miserably fails to do. My roommate already made her bed with a bright red comforter with geometric shapes outlined in black. A matching pillow sits at the headboard. A brightly-colored Picasso painting hangs above the brown dresser. Clothes are sticking out of the drawers, and there's empty candy wrappers scattered across the matching desk.

I don't belong here.

The thought comes before I can stop it, and I'm filled with a sinking dread. I walk a circle around the room. Maybe if my side wasn't so blank, it would feel better. I pull my bags inside the room and put the white and blue floral cotton sheets on the mattress. I lay my white eyelet comforter on top and then fold my small yellow, white, and blue floral quilt at the bottom of the bed.

Something is still off. I open my bag and pull out a gold framed photo of me and Chris, smiling into the camera. We took it at the lake over the summer. The memory of paddling out to the sandbar for a picnic lunch runs through my mind. I push the photo back into my bag and try to forget the happy faces. I pull out a matching frame, only this one has a photo of me, Teagan, and Ashling. We are all scrunched together on the front porch swing, laughing as Ashling makes a goofy face. A wave of homesickness hits me, and I hold the frame a little tighter before placing it on my wooden dresser. I would give anything to be back on that swing right now.

The door opens, and a girl with blonde and pink streaked hair walks in, laughing with a couple behind her. She stops when she sees me and frowns slightly.

"You must be Kayleigh." There's a note of annoyance in her tone.

"Hi. It's nice to meet you." I force a smile.

She doesn't look the least bit happy to meet me. "I'm Mona, and this Sophia and Leo. They're third years, but we all went to school together in San Diego."

"Oh, that's nice," I say, a little too enthusiastically. "I bet San Diego is just lovely."

Sophia lets out a snarky laugh. She stands there, arms crossed over her black lacy tank top. Her long dark hair has a deep purple tint when the light hits it, and her deep brown eyes are lined heavily.

"Lovely," Leo echoes. His greasy black hair hangs over his forehead as he runs his eyes over me. His pointed nose and barely-there mustache adds to his rat-like demeanor.

Sophia sends me a razor-sharp look before threading her arm protectively through his.

"So," I say, clearing my throat and turning to Mona, "you're an English major too, right?" I'm clutching at straws thinking of anything I know from our rooming assignments.

"Yes. Journalism." The clipped words tell me there's no more explanation coming.

"Me too." I hope my own words don't sound as deflated as I feel. "I'm looking forward to the newspaper. Just signed up a little while ago."

Mona throws Sophia a humorous look. "Sophia is the assistant editor of the paper."

Leo continues to stare at me, and I take the few steps to the window situated between our beds. I look out and remind myself that sometimes first impressions are wrong. I really hope so because if not, I can't image what my rooming situation will be this year.

"You *have* to have a hall party here tonight," Sophia says to Mona. It's a statement, not a question.

"I don't think—" I say, before Mona cuts me off.

"Yes!" She points at Sophia. "It'll be awesome."

"I don't think," I say again, searching my mind for any logical excuse to stop this, "we have a big enough room."

"You have an end room; it's bigger than most." Leo sits on my bed, and I have the sudden urge to do laundry.

"Let's go spread the word," Mona says, grabbing Sophia's hand and walking out.

Leo looks at me a moment longer before reluctantly getting up from my now wrinkled bedding and following them out the door. "See you tonight."

His voice raises the hairs on my neck.

Taking a deep breath, I look at the room, and disappointment settles in the pit of my stomach. This is not the roommate situation I was hoping for.

Just after dinner, people begin arriving for the party. Despite the constant movement of people coming in and out of the room, I sit at my desk, organizing my planner for the first week of classes. I crank up the classical piano music on my headphones, the noise-canceling element turned on, and try to drown out the heavy techno beat blaring from Mona's speaker.

As students wander back into the hallway, which is now streaming with people, it's only me and Mona in the room. She's adjusting the playlist, and I take the chance to talk with her privately, or at least as privately as possible.

"Mona," I say, taking off my headphones. "Aren't there RAs or something? I don't want to get in trouble." I worry that the resident advisor on our floor will write us all up, and it's not the way I want to start the year.

She gives me a look that makes me feel like I'm twelve years old. "Chill out. Sophia knows our RA."

Of course she does. Mona turns up the music and walks back into the hallway without waiting for my reply.

I feel the tears threatening, when my phone flashes with a new message from Teagan.

Finn and I are leaving for the festival. I know you're probably hanging out with your new roommate, but if you change your mind, we can pick you up on the way.

I almost jump out of my chair at the opportunity to get out of here. I type back as fast as I can.

I'd love to go with you guys! I'll be waiting outside. I throw my phone into my white leather envelope purse and sling it across my shoulder.

Before I can leave the room, Leo strides in reeking of alcohol.

"Hey." He winks a bloodshot eye at me.

"Get away from me." I push by him, and he stumbles, spilling his drink on my quilt.

I pull the door open and run down the hallway towards the exit. Out of the corner of my eye, I see Sophia watching me, fire in her eyes.

SEAMUS RIDES a gallant black stallion through the arena. He's clad in his full knight attire and holds his sword high as he thunders towards his opponent.

"The Knight of Kerry wins!"

The clansman falls dramatically from his horse, doing a somersault onto the sandy ground. The crowd cheers, and I laugh at the ridiculousness of it all.

I shake my head. "That was so fake," I whisper to Teagan, but realize she is jumping up and down along with the rest of the crowd.

Unbelievable. My practical and logical older sister is wrapped up in this show, which is more like a comedy routine than an actual duel or battle or whatever is actually going on here.

"Seamus is amazing as a Knight of Kerry," Teagan says when she finally sits back down.

"You don't think it's all kind of silly?"

She looks surprised at this. "Kayleigh, it's a show. It's supposed to be fun. I'm surprised you're not loving it."

I look away towards the concession stand. It is something I would normally love to watch, but seeing the men riding around on horses trying to save the maidan, while a nice fairytale, isn't what happens in the real world. And I'm tired of living in an imaginary world.

"I think sometimes a show or story distorts reality."

"Sure," she says drawing out the word, "but isn't that kind of the point?"

Is it the point? If more stories were based in reality would someone get so lost in a story that she doesn't see what's going on right in front of her? "I just think that there's no reason to fill people's minds with stories of love that will never happen in real life."

She takes a bite of a grilled turkey leg. "You are the most romantic person I know. You live for—"

"Love stories, right? Well, I was wrong. I don't think love is for me anyway." I give her a look that says there's no disputing this.

"See, I do think love is for you." Teagan returns my look with one of her own. "You, my forever romantic sister, just haven't met the right guy yet."

An image of Leo in my dorm room flashes through my mind. *Ugh.* If these are the guys out in the world waiting for me, then I prefer to avoid them all.

A bell clangs, and Seamus removes his helmet and chain mail hood. The crowd cheers him on as he holds out his hand to the beautifully gowned princess. She blushes as he kisses her gloved hand.

Forever romantic?

Not anymore.

AN HOUR LATER, as we walk towards the exit of the festival grounds, Seamus calls to us. He jogs over, still clad in his amor, and looks like he is still reveling in his recent win.

"Seamus!" Teagan gives him a side hug. "You were so good!"

"Really great." Finn high-fives him.

"Thanks. There's nothin' like a good ol' duel to win the princess."

"Right, knights are *so* amazing," I huff, sarcasm lacing each word.

"Ya like knights?" His grin verges on the cocky, completely missing my point.

"I'd take the horse over the knight these days."

He narrows his eyes. "Bollocks."

My hackles rise. "I'm realistic."

"Right." His expression says the complete opposite.

I glare at him. "I'm not the naïve romantic anymore," I say, emphasizing each word like that will change everyone's opinion of me.

His smile dims. "Sorry to hear that."

His words catch me off guard. "That's the last thing I expected you to say."

A look of disappointed crosses his face. "Nothin' wrong with bein' a romantic."

What does Seamus know about romance?

I shake my head. "Sure, in literature it's wonderful. But in real life, it's nothing but...a fairytale."

"Ya're in Ireland now. Fairytales are common."

"Now I'm sorry to hear that. Fairytales tell of imaginary happily ever afters and set people up for disappointment."

A gentleness mixes with the disappointment in his eyes. "Ya haven't met the right lad yet. That's all."

He sounds like Teagan. "And how would you know that?"

"Because once ya meet him, ya will believe in fairytales again."

"Are you speaking from experience?" There's an unexpected twinge of apprehension as I consider his answer.

His eyes don't leave mine. "A tale for another time, eh?" He begins to walk back to the arena.

"A tale is only as good as the lead character. Are you a strong character?" I call after him.

He turns and walks back, stopping just inches from me. "Are ya try'in to read me, Kayleigh?"

Heat prickles my cheeks at his proximity. "Would it be worth the read?"

"Every word." His eyes challenge me, and I don't dare turn away. There's something about him that stirs a deep longing in my soul. "See ya soon, Kayleigh O'Reilly."

He walks away, his armor gleaming in the moonlight, and I wonder what I just got myself into.

CHAPTER THREE

"When you write, write with feelin'. Yer heart should be poured out with each word."

As I sit in my Saints and Scholars core writing class, I have a flashback to sophomore year in British Literature with Mrs. Bello. The memory is of what I've always considered the beginning of my relationship with Chris. I shake the memory from my mind and try to concentrate on the professor at the front of the small lecture hall.

Professor Gaffney is in his mid-thirties with boyish dimples, strawberry blond hair, and freckled skin. Round gold-colored glasses highlight his bright green eyes. His youthful appearance is deceiving as it's already clear that he is wise beyond his years. His lectures the past couple of weeks have been brilliant. He is down-to-earth and energetic while lecturing, and strict and bold in his critiques. The latter is harder to take than I realized.

Being in the Saints and Scholars cohort is an honor, but one that brings with it more stress than energy. The course load is heavy and the expectations high. The stress of achievement is quickly overriding the need for sleep. I've always known that I want to be a writer, but burnout seems more likely right now. It's a disheartening way to begin my first year in university.

Professor Gaffney's face reddens with emotion. "If yer not writin' from the heart, then what's the point? Anyone can tell a story." He waves a dismissive hand. "My ol' Uncle James can weave a tale about anythin', but good luck to ya if ya stay awake. As writers we need to tell a story in a way that opens our hearts and allows readers inside to share in each heartbreak and triumph." He ascends a few steps in the lecture hall. "Will we inevitably leave readers brokenhearted and cursing us? Maybe. But, their hearts will never be the same."

His intensity is both inspiring and daunting. Don't I already pour my heart out in my writing? A moment's hesitation is all I need to know the answer.

"Professor Gaffney?" an alert girl in the front row asks, hand raised.

"What is it, Ms. Hanigan?" There's no annoyance in his tone, just curiosity. His focus is so intent that it's as if he waited all day for this one question.

"Do you think it's true that the brokenhearted are the best writers?"

He lets out a long, deep sigh. "That, Ms. Hanigan, is a question for the ages. I could quote Shakespeare or better yet Joyce or Yeats. I could tell ya that the Irish write beautifully from heartbreak."

There's a low chuckle at his obvious affinity for Irish writers.

"The answer lies in," he continues, "what ya do with that heartbreak. Heartbreak alone is not enough to make a great writer. It's what ya choose to do with that heartbreak that matters. Ireland has its fair share of heartbreak. Some are drowned in ale, but the smart ones drown their sorrows in literature. The ink is the blood they shed. So, which is it—the ale or the ink?" He asks this question to the class at large.

A murmur of voices fills the lecture hall, and his eyes land on me. He glances at a clipboard on his podium. "I didn't hear ya answer, Ms. O'Reilly. Would ya like to share ya thoughts on this question?"

"I'd prefer the ink." It's the obvious answer. I meet his eyes and continue, "But, I do think someone could be a good writer without necessarily opening his or her heart and bleeding, as you say, onto the page. If we're writers, then we should be able to get our message across with or without the proverbial blood."

A flash of what could only be described as pride crosses his face. "Aye, this is true. But, ya have missed the heart of it all."

I stare at him, confused about what he's implying.

"We're not just trying to be writers in here, Ms. O'Reilly," he says lowering his voice. The lecture hall is so quiet that I can hear the clock ticking on the side wall. "We're striving to become *extraordinary* writers. Which do you desire?"

"Ex-traordinary." I stumble on the word.

He nods at me and continues the lecture. I take notes while his question echoes in the back of my mind.

Which do I desire?

SAMARA and I walk out of the lecture, carrying our notebooks like they hold the answer to a professional writer career, or at least a top score in the course.

"He's intense," I comment, running my finger over at least ten used pages of my notebook. "I feel like I never stopped writing notes the entire hour, and I still missed things."

"I know what you mean. I've never been more thankful

for my dad's audio recorder than right now. I can send you the recording when I upload it." She nods to the rectangular black box on her notebook. "This thing was a lifesaver senior year."

"That would be great. Thanks."

"You seemed to catch his attention though." She gives me a quizzical glance. "I wonder if he'll ask you to be in Gaffney's Guild."

"What's Gaffney's Guild?"

"I heard that he often selects a few students from the program to join his writing group. Word is those students have all gone on to receive publishing deals. And the lucky ones, he publishes himself."

I stop abruptly, causing Samara to trip. "He's a publisher too?" I grab her arm to steady her.

Professor Gaffney's reputation as a writer is renowned. He's highly acclaimed, but I've never read anything about him being a publisher.

"Yup. He received some kind of large endowment and decided to use the money to start his own publishing house—Gaffney Press."

Professor Gaffney runs the Saints and Scholars program and his own publishing company. I can't help but wonder what I'd do with a large endowment. Is a publishing company Professor Gaffney's dream? As I continue walking down the hall, I wonder what my dream is. Is being a writer still my dream? Or is it another fairytale destined not to be a happily ever after?

We round the corner, and I collide with a man, spilling his large paper cup of coffee down the front of his crisp white polo shirt with the Emerald Isle logo embroidered on the left side chest.

"Ahh," he groans, pulling his shirt and steaming coffee away from his skin.

"I'm so sorry! Let me help you." I reach to take the envelope in his hands in hopes of minimizing the damage, but he pulls it back defensively.

"No! No need." His grip tightens around the envelope. I catch a brief glimpse of the Northern Ireland postage mark.

"Can I get you paper towels?" Samara asks.

"No need," he repeats as he brushes his shirt with his hand. A white and green name tag hangs on the pocket of his brown sports jacket.

"Oh, Mr. Banwell!" I exclaim.

"Do I know ya?" He shifts the bag from one shoulder to the other.

"I'm Kayleigh O'Reilly, Teagan's sister."

Recognition registers on his face as he takes a step backwards and bumps into another passing student. "Ah, sorry," he murmurs as the boy continues on his way.

"My sister told me so much about the science research program and the board of directors. We're so happy you all gave her and Finn a chance in the program."

His eyes dart to the floor. "Right. Well, they could hardly be blamed for the events of that summer."

"So true," I agree. "It was crazy—"

"Nice to meet ya," he interrupts. "I must be on my way."

We watch him hurry through the closest exit.

"That was odd," Samara murmurs.

Did I say too much? I think back over the events of two summers ago. "Maybe I shouldn't have brought up Teagan and Finn."

"Okay, what's going on?" She pulls me over to the two deep brown leather chairs in front of a corner window.

When we are seated I glance around. The hallway is practically empty now.

"Okay," I say quietly. "This has to stay between us."

Samara looks intrigued. "Of course."

"You know how I told you that Teagan and Finn came to Emerald Isle the summer after graduation to compete in the science research internship?"

"Yes, and their love story is one for the books."

"It really is. Well, there's a little more to it."

She leans closer to me. "I'm listening."

"When they arrived in Ireland, they learned about the legend of the Kildare emerald. A farmer was given a fifteen-carat Columbian emerald by his farmhand as a gesture of gratitude for giving his family a home and work. When the family moved back to Columbia, this farmer hid the emerald and a map on his land. The farmer, Eamon Kavanagh, was the father of Malachy Kavanagh, Teagan and Finn's mentor in the program."

"Did they find the emerald?" She squeals.

"Shh!" I remind her, and she covers her mouth. "Yes, they found it. And it saved the farm, which was having financial trouble, and the rest helped to fund their research program *Second Chances*."

"That's amazing."

"It is, but it wasn't easy, and they had to confront the Nathair gang in the process."

"Nathair? I've never heard of them."

"Nathair is Gaelic for snake. It's also the name of a notorious gang from the northern region. I've never seen them, but I hear that you will know it if you see 'em. Dressed all in black, they have a dark presence that sets them apart. That and matching tattoos on their forearms."

"What kind of tattoo?"

"A dark woven crown with thorns and a snake arching out of the top. Teagan said when you see it it's like the snake is looking straight at you, ready to strike."

"Sounds ominous."

"Yeah, well, they were trying to steal the emerald from the

Kavanaghs. Fiona, Teagan and Finn's mentor in the summer program, was in on it with her boyfriend, Ryan. Fiona's in jail now, but Ryan got away, and they don't know where he is. It's been quiet for the past year. The garda thinks they are laying low but that they will retaliate."

"Maybe they won't?" she asks hopefully.

"Maybe, but I think that may just be wishful thinking."

THE WHOLE GROUP meets at O'Callahan's the next day, and it's exactly how I pictured an authentic Irish pub. I glance into the mirrored glass of the door and adjust the sleeve of my baby blue princess-style blouse with billowy sleeves. My face is makeup free, and my long dark curls are pulled back with a loose ribbon at the nape of my neck.

"Over here!" Teagan calls to me from across the room.

I slide onto the chair next to her at the round dark wooden table. I greet Teagan's roommate, Zoey, on the other side of her. Zoey Campbell is a Montreal native with shoulder-length light blonde hair, friendly gray eyes, and a warm smile. They were assigned as roommates during their time at the university during the summer research program. Teagan really lucked out with her roommate. If only I could've been so lucky.

"Kayleigh, you remember Kyle, right?" Teagan gestures to the all-American football player from California sitting across the table next to Finn.

"Of course. Hi, Kyle."

He lifts a hand in greeting and offers a friendly smile. His curly blond hair is shorter than I remember, but his blue eyes are as welcoming as usual. Zoey and Kyle hit it off immediately during the summer program and became, as Teagan describes, "disgustingly cute" together. When our family visited Teagan shortly after final exams, Zoey and Kyle had broken up, and no one was talking about the reason.

A football game (soccer, not American football) plays on a television on the side wall. A group of university students are huddled in front of it, hurling insults at the opposing team's recent penalty.

"So, how's university life so far?" Kyle asks.

Where do I begin? "Um," I say tentatively, "not great actually."

I spend the next few minutes filling them in on everything going on, from my roommate to my classes. When I finish telling them about my run-in with Mr. Banwell earlier in the day, they all look confused.

"That's odd," Finn says. "It's usually hard to walk away from him because he's talking so much."

"Yeah, Finn and I were late to our organic chem lecture because he kept talking to us about rugby—which I actually would have preferred." Kyle swirls his pint before taking a gulp.

A low murmur of laughter fills our table.

"According to Kyle," Teagan explains to me, "chemistry is his nemesis."

"I'm with him on that one." I take a sip of my ale and allow the smoothness to run down my throat.

Zoey bites her bottom lip. "Although, I haven't seen Mr. Banwell around much lately."

Teagan takes a bite of her fried fish, considering this. "And I've never seen him out of the science wing."

"You know, that's true," Kyle says between bites of his corned beef sandwich. "Zoey and I actually just applied for a grant to study abroad in the Galapagos for our research." Him and Zoey exchange a small smile. "Our advisor said the application is just a formality at this point, but Mr. Banwell wasn't there to sign off on it."

Zoey nods. "His secretary said she would forward it along once he signed it."

"Well, we know he hasn't been on vacation on anything. And Kayleigh saw him today. How long ago did you apply?" Teagan asks.

"A week ago now," Kyle says, "and we still haven't heard anything from him or gotten the signed application back."

There's silence as this sinks in.

After a few moments, Zoey breaks the silence. "The trip would be amazing if it's approved though. We would be able to use our ecological engineering research to help with rewilding the native species."

"Rewilding?" I ask, realizing I am the only non-science person at the table.

"Yeah," Zoey continues, "it's a term used for returning lost species to their ancestral homes. We began looking into repairing ecosystems when we designed our summer research proposal at Overlook Point in County Clare."

I catch a look between Zoey and Kyle that tells me things may not actually be over between them.

"When would you leave?" Finn asks.

Kyle wipes his mouth. "Right after winter break."

"Right when we'll be needing the warmth the most." There's a hopeful look in Zoey's eyes.

Teagan watches her closely. "Sounds like a great opportunity for the *research*." She emphasizes the last word.

Zoey opens her menu. "I'm going to order an apple cake."

JUST AS WE'RE finishing dessert, Samara walks through the door, folding her umbrella.

"Samara, over here!" I call over the traditional Irish music coming from the band. Her black curls are more defined than usual and bounce as she makes her way to the table, sliding in next to Finn.

"It's like a monsoon out there." She removes her red rain jacket and drapes it on the back of her chair.

Seamus walks over to our table. It's the first time that I've seen him since the festival. His dark hair is damp, and he has a few days' worth of stubble on his face.

"Hey, man!" Kyle slaps his back goodheartedly. "Did your shift just start?"

"Aye, yer my first table tonight."

"Aww," Zoey coos, "lucky you."

He laughs. "I'm cuttin' you off."

He looks over at me, and our eyes meet. Heat travels through me, and I can't look away.

Samara clears her throat, and Seamus holds my gaze for another moment before turning to her.

"Samara, what'll ya have? The usual?"

"You know it."

"We have some ready. I'll bring it right out."

As Seamus walks back to the kitchen, I turn to Samara. "You have a usual already?"

"Of course. The shepherd's pie is amazing."

I laugh thinking about how easily Samara is now adjusting to Ireland. "It does sound good. How often do you come here?"

"Every night is a late night, and I seem to get more work done here than in the dorm."

I groan. "I understand that."

"I'm sorry," she croons. "Your roommate is worse, believe me."

Seamus places the steaming shepherd's pie in from of Samara. The marinaded beef smells delicious.

"Is it that bad?" There's concern in his eyes.

"Unfortunately, it's all too true." I rub my temples. "I

don't know how I'm supposed to get any writing done with their incessant noise and interruptions. I know they'd be happier without me too."

Acknowledging this stings more than I thought it would.

"I'd love to be your roommate," Samara says. "Maybe we could request a transfer or something."

Before I have time to consider this, Seamus pulls up a chair next to me. "I have a better idea. You can stay in my parent's cottage."

My mouth drops open. I know that Seamus' parents died when he was a child and to offer me their cottage is very generous. *But, would it be right to stay there? Is that infringing on family space?*

As if reading my mind, Seamus continues. "It's no trouble at all. I keep the cottage up to code and spend some time there, but I have my own flat now, so it's just sittin' there. Ya'd be doin' me a favor by usin' it and carin' for it."

I look to Teagan. She knows Seamus well and would give me her honest opinion.

She shrugs. "That sounds like it may be the answer you're looking for. I'm sure Mom and Dad will agree too."

Her words help to sooth any reservations. And honestly, I don't have many anyway. I would jump at any opportunity to get out of that room. "You're saving me, Seamus."

"Ah, come on now. I know you don't like bein' saved by any knights."

I flash him a challenging smile. "I think I can make an exception this one time." Then I remember Samara's offer. "Wait, Samara, maybe you could come too—"

"No worries." She holds up a hand. "While I'd love to move into a quaint Irish cottage, with my schedule, I would be back and forth too much. But, the cottage sounds like a perfect chance for you."

She's right. "I think it will be good for me to be alone for once." My excitement is growing. "And with my program schedule, I only have to be on campus three days, and the rest of the days I can work from the cottage. It should give me plenty of time for writing."

Seamus looks genuinely pleased at the idea. "The cottage is a quick trip to and from Dublin, especially if ya schedule ahead with the Cloverdale Trolley."

The thrill of living on my own wins the debate raging in my mind. "If you're sure, I'll take it."

"Ah," Samara squeals. "It's so romantic!"

"I don't know about romantic, but it is a good cottage," Seamus says quickly.

"And I don't need any romance in my life right now," I add, my voice firm.

Seamus nods in agreement before running a hand through his dark hair.

"I'll drive ya over in a bit to take a look." Seamus points out the window to his faded blue compact car parked on the street. It looks like it's seen better days.

"As long as you think it'll make it." I squint to get a better view.

"Don't ya worry about ol' Jemma, she's grand."

"Jemma?" I ask.

The others try to hide their smiles while Samara looks as confused as I am.

"The car." He looks at me like I'm the one who has lost my mind.

"I can't believe you named your car," I say between giggles.

"Ya want a ride or not? The cottage is fine on its own, mind ya."

I pull myself together quickly. "No! I definitely want the cottage. And if Jemma," I say, forcing a neutral expression, "is the way to get there, I'm happy for the ride. Please tell her I say, thank you."

His mouth reluctantly pulls up at the side. "I'll let her know."

As he walks back to the kitchen, we all burst out laughing.

———

WHEN WE PULL up in front of Seamus' flat, I look up at the five-story red brick building. It is well-maintained and free of the debris that is so common in a city.

"Rent prices are outrageous, so I bought this flat a little while back. Lookin' at it as an investment. It's walkin' distance to the docks, and I can see *Crossways*." He looks towards the water.

"Crossways?"

A smile teases his lips.

"Let me guess. The name of your boat?"

The smile is full-on now. "Aye. Named it after—"

"Yeats' first collection of poetry."

Surprise registers in his expression. "A fan of poetry, are ya?

"Yes," I say, leaning back into the seat. "I can imagine a poem could win the hearts of many."

"Would a poem win your heart?" His question is light, but there's something deeper in the way that he asks.

I watch a car drive by. "My heart isn't open to the chance."

A frown creases his strong mouth. "That's a tragedy if I ever heard one. Yer heart would be worth fightin' for."

My heart says, "fight for me," while my mind warns, "he can break your heart." My silence lasts a moment too long, and Seamus turns off the engine and gets out of the car. The sound of the door closing echoes in my heart.

There's a click of the handle, and then Seamus mumbles

to himself. He tugs and twists on the handle as he fights with the lock. "Come on, ya bugger!"

His wiggles the handle up and down and then pushes his body against the door. He gives it three full-body pushes before I can't hold my laughter any longer. He stops and stares at me through the smeared window, perspiration dotting his forehead. As I struggle to control myself at the ridiculous sight of a grown man fighting with a door, he walks back around to the driver's side.

"Alright, just climb out this side."

"You are quite the dashing knight," I tease. "Although, I think you may need a new horse." I wink at him before I climb out and walk to the apartment steps.

"She's grand." He follows me. "Just needs a little work, that's all."

"Whatever you say, Lancelot."

We stop on the third floor, and Seamus opens the door to a single bedroom flat. As I enter, I'm greeted with a full floor-to-ceiling library. I walk straight over to it and browse the various volumes.

"Your book collection is amazing."

"The one thing I knew I couldn't live without when I moved in here was a library. Some of my favorites are from when I was a lad." He looks longingly at a section of old leather-bound books.

"Did your parents have a library?" I ask cautiously. Seamus obviously cared for his parents very much, and losing them at such a young age had to be hard. I shudder to think what would've happened if he didn't have the Kavanaghs.

"Aye." Fondness warms his voice. "We had a grand one. Ma and Dad would read every night. We'd choose a book, and I would sit by the fire as they took turns readin'. Some of my fondest memories."

"That's why you love literature so much today."

"I can't deny that. Yeats was their favorite. Never went a day without hearing a line or two."

I step closer and pick up a black framed photo of a woman and man smiling at the camera, the sea at their backs. The woman laughs as the wind blows her ginger hair about, a few strands crossing her green eyes. While the man has an arm wrapped around her shoulders and a contented smile on his face—a face that is so similar to the man next to me that it's hard to tell who's who. The same unruly dark hair and intriguing hazel eyes that seem to look right into your soul. The photo emits pure happiness. His parents were very much in love, and there's no doubt that their small family shared many happy memories together. It must have broken Seamus' heart when they passed away.

"They look like wonderful people." I place the photo back on the shelf.

Seamus follows my gaze. "They were the best."

I consider the best way to approach the topic of their deaths. "Teagan mentioned there was an accident at sea."

"Aye, the Dublin Bay. Da had this idea that the best fish could be caught right before a storm. They were needin' the money and took a chance. Da was right about the fish. They were out and bitin'. Turns out a drop of barometric pressure and low sunlight causes the fish to feed more aggressively. Da didn't know that though, just followed his instincts. He was a natural fisherman. And Ma never left his side, not even that mornin'."

I put a hand on his arm. "They got caught in the storm?"

His nods. "They were less than a kilometer to shore when the waves took 'em under."

"I'm so sorry."

"The east winds were blowin' that day. They're notorious for shipwrecks 'round here." He gets a faraway look in his eyes. "I was home at the cottage. It was past mid-mornin', and I knew they should've been back by then. I watched the bay for any sign of the boat before finally closin' the shutters because of the wind. Somehow I knew they were gone. I didn't need the garda to confirm it when they came later that afternoon. Bits of the boat washed up on shore, but their bodies were never found."

"I can't imagine what that was like for you." I picture Seamus as a young boy, standing by the window waiting for his parents, but they never return.

He stares off into the distance. "After their deaths, a part of me was glad their bodies weren't found. They belong to the sea, just like me."

My heart aches for Seamus and the boy he was. To lose both parents in a single day could be too much for some, but he made it through—probably with the help of the community surrounding him. "Is that when the Kavanaghs took you in?"

"Aye. Uncle Malachy and Aunt Nora saved me from what I'm sure would've been a very different path for me. I went to live with them on the farm, but we kept the cottage, and as I got older I spent more and more time there. It was like having them back in a way."

My initial doubts return about the cottage. "Are you sure you want me to stay there? I really don't want to intrude on your family's home."

"Ah, blarney. Ya're not intruding on anythin'. My folks would've loved havin' ya stay. And I do too."

I feel color rising to my cheeks. "Well, I feel honored to stay there."

I realize my hand is still on his arm. I know I should pull it away, but I don't. I like being close to him and don't want to break our connection.

When I finally allow my hand to fall, I take in the rest of the space. A brown leather sofa and perpendicular loveseat flank a driftwood coffee table, holding a book on ancient ships and a collection of Yeats' works. Navy blue and cream-colored throw pillows are scattered about with a green Aran wool blanket thrown across the back of the sofa. There's a coziness that invites you to sit and stay awhile.

The small kitchenette is clean and bright with its white walls and stainless steel appliances. A tea kettle sits on the stove awaiting the warmth of a brew.

Seamus shuts the corner drawer of the cabinet and checks a small blown glass tray on the counter for a second time. "I must've left the key on the boat. It's a quick walk, if ya don't mind."

I shiver at the unexpectant cool breeze that flutters through the slightly ajar window. "Oh, right. No, I don't mind."

"Here, this'll keep ya warm." He holds open his olive waxed jacket. "The temperatures drop quickly after sunset, and the breeze off the water brings a chill."

I slide my arms into the jacket. Our faces are just inches apart. The warmth of his jacket and the faint scent of the salty sea has me questioning whether I don't still believe in love after all, but I push the thought away.

"Ready?" I walk out the door without waiting for his answer.

WHEN WE REACH THE DOCK, flood lights illuminate dozens of boats, all varying in color, tied to rigs along the side. I follow him to one with the lower side painted blue and the top side white, with a matching blue roof on the galley. The paint appears new, and there's minimal chipping along the edges. *Rocky Shore Fishing* is in red bold lettering on the sides, and *Crossways* is centered in script on the rear board. Light reflects off the ragged edges of the glass windows.

Wait, ragged edges?

Seamus says something I don't catch and climbs onboard. He mutters to himself as he examines the broken window of the captain's cabin.

I follow him onto the boat, gripping the rail for balance. Gentle waves lap around us swaying the boat from side to side. Pieces of glass slide back and forth across the smooth floor.

Seamus is standing at the helm, mouth agape as he examines the controls.

Pieces of metal from the gaskets are strewn about while the steering wheel is lying face down in a puddle of water. Wires are cut from the dashboard, and dials hang from their remaining cords.

"Who would do this?"

"Someone who's tryin' to put me out of business." His jaw clenches. "And somethin' tells me this is only the beginning."

CHAPTER FOUR

A week later, I wake to the rain sounding on the thatched cottage roof. I turn over in bed and pull my quilt tighter around myself. Just as I begin falling back to sleep, my phone rings, and Ashling and Teagan's photos pop up on the screen. I pull myself up and rest my back against the wooden headboard before answering the video call.

"Alright, let's see this cottage," Ashling says without hesitation.

I slide my feet into my slippers. "I'll start with the bedroom, since I was peacefully sleeping until the phone rang."

"Come on, Kayleigh, you know that a solid morning routine sets the tone for the whole day." Teagan is bright-eyed and lively in her bright blue tank top. Her long, straight black hair is pulled into a ponytail that hangs over her shoulder, and her normally fair cheeks are ruddy.

"Did you just finish a workout?"

"I just ran a couple of miles around campus. There was a beautiful sunrise today."

I glance out the window. "It's raining."

"Well, it is now. You missed it. It was glorious."

Ashling snickers. "Okay, as fun as this is, it's two in the morning here, and Mom says I need to actually go to school tomorrow."

Teagan pulls her phone closer to herself. "What do you mean 'actually go?'"

Ashling tucks a strand of auburn hair behind her ear. "Kayleigh, show us the cottage. I'm on the edge of my seat over here."

Her obvious change of subject is concerning, but it's a little too early for me to take a standing ground like Teagan. We'll circle back to that another time.

I climb out of bed and scan around the room, showing them the quaint bedroom with white painted walls and ceiling with aged wooden beams. My yellow and blue quilt and flowered sheets look right at home in the cozy ambience of the room. A rocking chair sits in the corner with a hand-woven blue pillow. I walk out into the short hallway and peak quickly into Seamus' room. There are the same cream-colored walls, but the bed has a darker hue to the wood making it a bolder sight. A deep red and blue knitted blanket is spread out over tan sheets. The bed is neatly made, and I wonder when the last time Seamus slept here.

I close his door and show them the sitting room and connected kitchen and dinette. Everything about the cottage speaks of a life well-lived and joyful homemaking. Family photos are hung throughout the cottage in a way that feels comforting but not overwhelming. I grab my raincoat and walk through the red front door to show them the exterior. The white hardened clay base stands out against the surrounding rolling green hills. The straw-colored thatched roof slopes down as if hugging the frame. Two open-framed windows sit on either side of the door.

"It's so cute," Teagan says. "Just perfect for you."

"It really is," I agree. I couldn't have designed a home more perfect.

"What's the view from those windows?" Ashling asks.

I turn around and point the phone facing the sparkling blue waters of the Dublin Bay. A planked wooden dock jets out from the rocky sand shore.

"Oh, wow." Teagan's eyes widen. "It's beautiful."

"Yeah, incredible. It's like your own private island."

I smile at Ashling's description. "I know. I can't thank Seamus enough for this." I turn the phone around to face me. "I wasn't sure how long I was going to last at Emerald Isle with the dorm situation and all, but now I feel like I have a chance."

"It's so good to see you happy again," Teagan says, taking a sip of a green smoothie.

"Yeah, and with Chris, I know it has to be hard." Ashling's comment catches me off guard. She rarely says things like this, and I know she never cared for Chris.

"The breakup was really hard, and it's still a bit of a shock, but I like being on my own right now,"I assure her.

"That's a relief. I wasn't sure how you would take the news."

I pause at Ashling's words. *What news?*

"Wait, what news?" Teagan asks, echoing my thoughts.

Ashling shrugs. "About Chris and Tori. If you ask me, they belong together like all scum does."

Chris and Tori are together? I expect feelings of betrayal and jealousy, but instead I don't feel anything.

After a few beats of silence and seeing our shocked expressions, Ashling continues. "I'm sorry, Kayleigh. I thought you knew. It's all over social media."

"I gave up social media when I left for Ireland. Fresh start and all." I'm so grateful for that decision now.

"It doesn't matter, right Kay," Teagan says will a forced

brightness in her tone. "That's the past, and you're focusing on the present and the future." Teagan never joined social media, citing it too distracting from her work, so this must be a shock to her too.

I feel like I'm back in high school again, focusing on Chris and our relationship. Or in this case, our nonexistent relationship. The unusual feeling of anger begins to boil again as I consider how much time I wasted on Chris.

"The truth is," I finally say, "I have more important things going on than to worry about what Chris is or isn't doing."

There's an audible sigh of relief from Teagan.

"Let's talk about something else." I close the front door behind me.

"Dolly got loose and ran down Main Street again. You should've seen her go. I think this was her fastest run yet." Ashling mimics our crazy pig's squeal.

My mind drifts as she recounts the story in a way only Ashling can. I stretch out on the faded red linen sofa, pulling a large gold goose down pillow under my head. The image in my mind of Chris and Tori fades to Seamus' smile. That smile is one that's hard to forget.

A knock sounds at the door. I peak out the window and see Seamus standing there in a green Republic of Ireland national football team hoodie. His hands are in his pockets, thumbs tapping against his jeans.

I quickly run my fingers through my bed-mused hair and tuck my pink long-sleeved thermal top into my white and green plaid pajama bottoms. *Do I have time to change?*

"Earth to Kayleigh." Ashling's voice brings me back to the conversation with my sisters. "What's going on?"

I run my fingers through my messy hair one last time, trying to loosen the remaining knots. "Seamus is here."

"Well, that explains it." Ashling laughs.

"Ashling, don't start. He's just a friend."

Their expressions tell me that neither of them believes me. "Listen, I'll call you guys back later."

I end the call as another knock sounds. "Kayleigh, are ya in there?"

When I open the door, I can't help the emotions that swirl within me. Excitement, joy, nervousness, apprehension.

"Hi," I say, trying for nonchalance, but not quite achieving it. "You look great."

You look great? Seriously, what is wrong with me?

His eyebrow quirks with amusement.

"I mean, you look healthy. You know, in your prime. Thanks to all those days on the boat, no doubt." *Stop. Just stop.* "Your doctor must be proud."

Okay, I'm the one who needs a doctor, or better yet, a psychologist.

"He is a good doctor." Seamus tries unsuccessfully to hide his grin. "Ya look cute too by the way."

Argh. My pajamas. I wish I could turn back time and start all over.

This time I can't find any words, so I just stand there staring at him. I'm not sure what's worse, my mindless talking or uncontrolled staring.

"So." He breaks the silence, looking very amused. "I was just stoppin' by to see if ya want to go to the Cloverdale Market this mornin'."

"Oh." Again with the brilliant words. This is clearly an example of my skill as a writer. "I'd love to." I glance down at my pajamas. "Just let me change first."

I run into the bedroom and close the door behind me. *Pull yourself together.*

I quickly wash up in the attached powder room and slip on a long white cotton sundress with green belt and blue jean jacket. The rain has slowed to barely a mist, and the sun is beginning to peak from the clouds.

"I'm goin' to work on the leaky faucet," Seamus calls to me. The sound of running water travels down the hallway.

I apply a shimmery light blue eye shadow and navy mascara to my eyes. I slide on dangling sterling silver flower earrings, swipe a few strokes of rose-colored blush on my cheeks, and add matching gloss for my lips.

That's better.

When I join Seamus in the kitchen, he's under the sink tightening a screw on the pipe.

"I'm ready when you are."

"Just finished." He scoots out of the cabinet and does a double take. "Wow, you look incredible."

My cheeks deepen in color. "Thank you. And thanks for fixing the facet. The dripping was driving me crazy."

He gives me another look of appreciation before returning the tools to the back cabinet. "We best be goin'."

He holds the cottage door open for me. "After ya, m'lady."

WHEN WE ARRIVE at the market, people are milling around the town square. There's still a dampness in the air, but the rain is holding off. The market preserves the old simplicity and comfort of another era. Being in Cloverdale is like stepping back in time, while showing me what my future could look like.

"Teagan!" I wave to my sister, who's shifting through a produce bin.

She pays for her apples and jogs over to us. "Hey! I didn't realize you guys were coming today." She gives us each a hug, while throwing me a knowing look. A blue jean dress has replaced her blue tank top, but her hair is still pulled back into a ponytail.

I nod to Seamus. "Seamus says it's the best place to pick up local food and meet the townspeople."

Teagan laughs. "You will definitely get to know the people here." She looks around fondly and points to a middle-aged man with red hair and a woman with black curls. "You'll want to stop over there. Mr. and Mrs. Walsh make the best butter in the entire county. Seriously, you'll have to pick up some for the cottage."

"Right about that," Seamus agrees.

I look between the two of them. They both have a contented air to them, like they've already found what they're looking for.

"I see you are quite the local now." I playfully nudge Teagan.

Her lips form a peaceful smile. "I guess I am."

"I see ol' man Smith is at the gab today. I'm goin' to go save Finn." Seamus walks in the direction of the two men, leaving me and Teagan to wander around on our own.

"You two seem to be growing close." Teagan glances at me between the racks of herbs.

"Like I said, we're friends."

Teagan ignores this. "The good news is that the money you're saving on the dorm can cover the rent for the cottage, and you'll probably still have a good amount left over." She's considering the situation in her meticulous way. "It's a great benefit to living off campus."

The truth is that Seamus didn't want to charge me anything for rent. He finally agreed to after Mom and Dad insisted they speak to him. They would not take no for an answer and said if he wouldn't accept the money for the cottage alone then to use it for his fishing business.

While Teagan lived with the Kavanaghs for most of her internship last summer, she moved into the dorm with Zoey for the school year. "Do you miss being off campus?" I ask.

"Sometimes. But for now, it's good to be at the university. It makes it so much easier for Finn and me to work on the research and study for our classes. The library is there, and the computers in the research center are so much better with the data computation than what we could do on our own."

"And you get to live with Zoey, which I'm sure is nice." The smallest twinge of sadness hangs on my words.

Teagan turns to me. "I'm sorry the roommate situation didn't work out for you. It really was bad luck."

Maybe. But, it feels like a good thing it didn't work out.

"I guess." I twirl a flower stem between my fingers. "Although, I think the cottage is a better fit for me anyway."

"I agree." Teagan threads her arm through mine, and we continue browsing the market.

As we stroll the grounds, stopping at various tables, I feel more and more confident that this is where I'm meant to be. I pick up a glass spray bottle with a hand-lettered paper label. *Lavender Water*. I mist my wrist and take in the delicate floral scent. It's light and fresh, and I spritz another mist on my other wrist.

"That's my favorite one too." A slender woman with a long brunette braid hanging over her shoulder gestures to the bottle in my hands. She appears to be in her late twenties or early thirties, her complexion shining in a bright yellow cotton dress and purple cardigan with lacy embroidered flowers. "Lavender produces the most incredible herbal scent. It blends well with orange blossom, bergamot, and patchouli, among others."

I smell my wrist again. It's the perfect blend of light floral and calming essence. There are a few lavender buds floating in the water. "I love it. And the bottle is precious."

"My brother makes the bottles. He has a special gift for blowin' glass and workin' with metal."

I examine the intricately detailed glass rim and smooth rounded edges of the metal cap. "He's an artist."

"Indeed he is. I'm Laoise." She stretches out a hand to me and then Teagan.

"I'm Kayleigh, and this is my sister, Teagan."

"Of course. Ye look like twins."

"That's what everyone says," I tell her.

"I love this orange blossom scent." Teagan mists herself.

"The two scents complement each other very well." She looks between the two of us. "I always wanted a sister. The Lord gave me five brothers instead."

"Five?" Teagan and I ask in unison.

She laughs. "Aye. Three older and two younger. Cormac, the youngest, is the one who made these glass bottles."

"Wait, Cormac? There's a Cormac joining us at Brigid's Crossing as farrier," Teagan said.

"That's him! We're so proud for him to have that job. Cormac's had a rough go of it. This is the break he needs."

Unanswered questions hang in the air between us as we take in her words.

"Well, Brigid's Crossing is the place for second chances," Teagan says. "And I'm looking forward to working with him."

"He's a good lad, and his artistry can't be denied. Although, I need to remind myself that eighteen isn't a lad anymore."

We all admire the glass bottles again before Teagan and I buy our fragrances and continue walking around. Finn and Seamus join us, each of them carrying a bouquet of wildflowers.

"These are beautiful!" I run my thumb over the soft petals of a purple bell heather.

Teagan smells her bouquet. "Caitlin Mahoney started collecting flowers by the cottage last summer and now has the cutest nursery and garden in the area. She brings her flowers to the market, and they are always gone in the first couple of hours."

Caitlin, her husband, Sean, and their grandson, James, helped Teagan and Finn last summer in the hunt for the emerald. It was Caitlin's words that Teagan took to heart and then discovered where the map was buried. Then it was James' comment about the emerald not being buried in the ground that helped lead them to the treasure in the old tree.

"She has wonderful taste. I love wildflowers and these are the most beautiful ones I've ever seen." I bask in the sweet scent before catching Seamus' eye. He's watching me with a slight curve to his mouth.

"They will go perfect on the kitchen table in the cottage," I say, still holding his gaze.

"Right ya are. They're perfect." His eyes linger on me for another moment.

We are sampling the rosemary and lavender shortbreads when a rumble tears through the air. Four men, dressed all in black, drive their motorbikes up to the entrance. The bustle of the market silences as vendors and villagers watch them convene at the brewery stand.

Teagan holds her breath beside me.

The men take their pints and gulp them down in one swig before dropping them on the cobblestone street. The sound of glass shattering causes gasps from the villagers.

Mayor McCarthy sets his bowl of beef stew on a nearby table and walks briskly towards the men. "Hold on right now. Ye need to do some explaining.'"

The men stare at him as wicked grins spread across their faces. The largest man takes a step forward as the other three flank him. "Explainin' for what?" He lets out an amused laugh.

"The mess ye just made. These are good people, spendin' their hard-earned bob to make this market what it is. Ye can't go 'round carelessly breakin' their mugs. And the glass can cut the wee ones runnin' about. What were ye thinkin'?" He stands squared off to the man.

"I don't like this," Teagan murmurs as Seamus and Finn return to our sides.

Seamus stands slightly in front of me in a protective gesture. "Me neither."

The large man cracks his knuckles one by one before taking two steps closer to Mayor McCarthy, whose stark white complexion is now a shade lighter than his already fair skin.

"We need to do something," Finn says.

"Yeah," Teagan agrees, "but what?"

Before we can decide the best action, the man wraps a meaty hand around Mayor McCarthy's neck and lifts him into the air.

Some of the villagers begin shouting at him to stop. Any potential help is blocked off at his sides.

"This town is changin'. Time for ya to get on board or get out!"

Mayor McCarthy grabs at his neck and mutters something that we can't understand.

"Ya need to learn respect. I'll let it go this time." The man gives a wicked snarl. "But, I won't be so kind next time." He throws the mayor to the ground. Then he and the other men walk pointedly back to their motorbikes and speed off.

The crowd rushes to the mayor's side and quickly help him to sit upright. He rubs the swollen red welts around his neck. This town cares for each other. The similarity to our home in Berryville is unmistakable, and I feel a protectiveness for these people, even though I haven't been here for long.

"It's Nathair I tell ya. They're goin' to be the end of us." I recognize the older woman as the baker's wife. Tears slide down her rosy cheeks.

"It won't be the end of us," her husband says, wrapping an arm around her. "They can't take everything away from us."

"That's right," Malachy adds. He and Nora walk over from their jam stand. "We'll never go down without a fight."

"What can we do?" Finn asks.

"There's nothin' we can do yet." Nora holds up a hand. "Apart from an assault charge, there's nothin' much keepin' 'em away."

"They are set on takin' over this town." Mayor McCarthy's voice is raspy but strong.

Malachy takes off his cap and wipes his forehead before replacing it. "That won't happen with the board in place."

"Aye. Let's just pray the board stays intact." Mayor McCarthy stands with the help of two men. He looks around at the small crowd, tenderness in his eyes. "I will do everythin' I can to make sure it does."

"And we'll be right there with ya," Liam Dunne, the burly blacksmith, says.

They act more like family than merely neighbors. They are all invested in the same thing. They want this town to remain as it is. People will often say that change is necessary, and that whether good or bad, change brings about new beginnings. While that is true, I can't help but want to preserve the authenticity and dynamic of this small town.

The townspeople continue strolling the vendors' tables and conversing with each other. There is laughter overriding the tension in the air. A plump lady brings Mayor McCarthy another bowl of beef stew, which he immediately sits down to enjoy. My surprise must be evident because Teagan lays her hand on my shoulder and leans close.

"We can't hide in fear of Nathair," she whispers.

I turn to her. Her crystal blue eyes, so like my own, hold only the faintest hint of worry. "How can you be so calm? How can everyone be so calm?"

Teagan sighs. "I know. I used to feel the same way. But, being here I've learned that we can't control everything, even as much as we may want to."

I look at her, amazed at how much she has grown over the past year. She has a contentedness to her that she didn't have before coming to Ireland.

"But," she continues, "we will continue to plan for their attack and—"

I cut her off. "You think they will attack the town?"

Her lips form a thin line. "Yes. Although, not necessarily a physical battle. No one knows how the attack will come, but there's little doubt that it will come. I know the Irish people never back down from defending something they believe in. Cloverdale may be a small town compared to cities like Dublin, but the people have conviction and faith."

She points down the street to St. Patrick's, the small stone chapel in the heart of the town.

"Towns were originally built around a central place of worship, and it wasn't until coming to Ireland that I understood why."

"Because faith is the center of everything." My voice is flat, without emotion.

"Exactly."

When was the last time I prayed or even considered my faith? Sure, at home I went to church most Sundays with my family, but beyond that, what was my relationship with God?

I shift on my feet because I know the answer. I don't have a relationship at all right now. My faith has always been there, but it is weak and a severely wounded one recently.

Seeming to sense my internal dilemma, Teagan touches my arm, and we stop walking. "Why don't you come to Mass with us tomorrow? The Kavanaghs have these big Sunday dinners around noon after Mass. At first, I couldn't believe they went through all of that work every week, but now I see how the Sunday dinners are not just about the food but bringing people together."

A feeling I can't put my finger on has me agreeing. "Okay. That would be nice."

"What would be nice?" Seamus asks. He and Finn look at us expectantly.

"Mass and Sunday dinner tomorrow."

"*Right*." Seamus draws out the word.

"Malachy and Nora always ask about you and say they hope you'll come one week." Finn gives him a hopeful look.

"Maybe one week." The insincerity is clear in his tone. I don't think even Seamus believes it.

"Tomorrow," I say, a note of finality in my voice. "We'll go together."

Seamus looks like a mouse before the cat pounces.

"No excuses." I point my finger at him. "You are my ride after all."

"I guess I don't have a choice then." His dry humor makes me smile.

"No, you don't," I tease.

Teagan clears her throat. "Alright, time for us to go." She takes Finn's hand. "We'll see you tomorrow!"

They walk towards the path leading back to Brigid's Crossing. I look back at St. Patrick's and wonder what tomorrow will bring.

CHAPTER FIVE

We're quiet on our drive back to the cottage. I stare out the window, the scene from the market running through my mind. If Nathair is as big of a threat to the community as it appears, there has to be something we can all do to prevent it. I run through possibilities but come up short for a practical idea. This is really Teagan's area. How she hasn't come up with something yet surprises me. As we drive up the curved path to the cottage, I spot movement by the rose bush.

"Seamus, stop!" I hit his arm, and he slams on the breaks. The car squeals and a few paper bags spill onto the floor from the back seat.

"What are ya doin'?" He throws his hands up in air. "Ya tryin' to hurt Jemma?"

"Jemma's just fine!" I pull the door handle, but it won't release. I push against the door with my shoulder, giving enough leverage to pop the door open. "I think your Jemma needs a face lift or a replacement altogether."

"She didn't mean it," Seamus coos to the car. "She's American."

There's a whimper as a massive dog's tail thumps on the ground. Even with the matted fur and dirt, his size and demeanor takes my breath away. Although his rancid stench may be adding to that.

"What kind of dog are you?" I ask the dingy animal.

"A mess is what he is."

I roll my eyes and hold my hand out to the dog. He smells it once before covering it with slobbery kisses. "Don't mind him. He's Irish."

"Funny." Seamus squats down next to him, and the dog eyes him suspiciously.

"Colonel, be nice."

Seamus lets out a laugh. "Colonel? Ya've named him already?"

"Of course. Every dog needs a name. And this one is a gentleman. Honorable, dignified, chivalrous, and loyal."

Seamus looks back at the matted dog. "If ya say so."

"He just needs a bath."

"I think he needs more than a bath."

I walk over to the side of the cottage, Colonel and Seamus following behind. I peek through the window and into the bathroom.

"What are ya doin' now?"

"Trying to gauge if the tub is big enough for him."

"Ah, no ya don't." He shakes his head, eyes growing wide. "That thing is not goin' in there."

"Colonel," I say pointedly, "needs a bath—"

"And Colonel can have that bath outside instead of ruinin' my tub."

I exhale a long breath. Okay. Seamus may have a point. "Fine. I'll get the soap, and you get a bucket and the hose."

"You want the dog, but *I* need to clean him?"

"Yup! You're helping me."

Seamus just stares at me as I gently shake Colonel's shoulder. At some point during our debate, he curled up on the grass and fell asleep.

"Come on, boy, time for a bath."

The dog gives a big yawn and stretches his long legs.

When he licks my face, I giggle but push him away. "No! Don't try sweet talkin' me; you are in desperate need of a bath."

I rub his matted ears and turn to Seamus. "You'll see. Beneath all this mess, there's a gentle and noble soul in there."

Seamus' eyes soften as he watches us. "Come on. Let's clean him. I don't know how much longer I can take his smell."

I smile into Colonel's fur before coaxing the large dog up and over to the outdoor water spicket before grabbing my body wash from the shower.

"This will have to do." I hand Seamus the bottle of lavender wash. "I know he may smell like flowers, but it's all I have."

He adds soap to the bucket and swishes it around until it's a soapy mixture. Colonel must sense what's about to happen because he takes one look at the hose and turns to run. Seamus catches him before he bolts and slides a rope around his neck.

"Is that necessary?" I ask, eyeing the rope.

"Aye. Unless you want him running and never comin' back."

I frown but see his reasoning. "Alright, but we need to get him a proper collar and leash soon."

Seamus looks like he's about to say something but thinks better of it. He rubs the soap into Colonel's fur and scrubs through the knots. He takes clippers to the mats that don't wash out and then hoses him down.

After drying him as best we can, we go inside to sit by the fire. Colonel stretches out, lolled to sleep by the warmth.

"Kayleigh," Seamus says seriously, "what are ya goin' to do with him?"

I watch Colonel close his eyes, fully comfortable in his place in the cottage. I can't leave him outside. He deserves a good home, and something tells me that this is it. "I'm going to keep him." I suddenly remember that this is Seamus' cottage, and I'm overstepping my rights. "If that's okay with you."

He shrugs. "I don't think I could say no to ya if I wanted."

My heart leaps, whether from Seamus' words or the fact that I now have a new dog, I'm not sure. "He'll be my guard dog. I am all alone out here. It will be nice to know he's with me."

A flash of jealousy crosses Seamus' face. "Great protector he is."

Colonel rolls over onto his back, legs stretched high into the sky.

THE NEXT EVENING, after a comforting bowl of Irish stew, I curl up on the sofa with my laptop. It's time to get back into the story that I'm developing for Professor Gaffney's class. As I wait for the document to load, I notice a notification in my inbox. I click on my email folder, and a message from Professor Gaffney pops up.

I quickly scan the message, and my heart sinks. As if delivering a second blow, my working manuscript pops up onto the screen. The words swim together in a muddled mess. I wipe a runaway tear from my eye before slamming my laptop shut.

Nothing in my life is working out the way I dreamed.

I get into the shower, hoping the water can erase Professor Gaffney's words from my mind. When the hot water runs out, I step out of the shower with only one thing on my mind—I need to get out.

I pull on a pair of blue jeans and a black long-sleeve top and leave my hair down, the curls still damp. The taxi arrives a few minutes later, and after a short drive I'm back in Dublin and headed straight for O'Callahan's pub.

"Kayleigh!" Seamus' familiar voice calls out to me from down the street.

I don't turn around and pick up my pace instead.

Seamus catches up to me. "What are ya doin'?"

I stop just outside the pub door and turn to him. "I'm going to wash my sorrows away. Isn't that what you do in Ireland after all."

He puts a hand over the door handle. "Ya don't want to do that."

"I am so sick of people telling me what I do and don't want. How do you know what I want?"

"I wish I knew what ya want." There's a yearning in his tone. "But I can tell ya from experience that ya don't want that." He jabs a thumb towards the pub.

My jaw tightens. "I don't know what I want."

Seamus takes my hand and pulls me in the opposite direction of the pub. When we reach his car, he opens the door and waves his hand at the empty passenger seat. "Go on, Jemma awaits."

"Only if you tell me where you are taking me."

"Far away from the pub," he murmurs more to himself than to me. "I'll take ya back to the cottage."

"I don't want to go back yet." I cross my arms over my chest.

He lets out a long exasperated sigh. "Listen, whatever ya need, ya won't find it in the pub."

I know he's right, and I sit in the passenger seat feeling both angry and relieved. He starts the engine, and we're driving on the back road within minutes. He glances at me every once in a while but doesn't say anything.

"My writing professor for the Saints and Scholars program thinks my writing..." I think back to the words he used, "is superficial and lacking in heart."

He lets my words sink in before speaking. "Is he right?"

"What? No, of course not!" I shake my head and look out the window and into the darkness.

Is he right? I never even considered it until now. I think about the short story I submitted. I wrote about a woman who, following a terrible divorce, traveled to Italy to start her life over. The similarity to my own life has to assure it was heartfelt. There are doubts lingering in my mind. I think back to sitting on my bed and writing it in a couple of hours the day before it was due. It flowed easily, almost automatically.

Like a robot.

When we pull up to the cottage, I turn to Seamus. "Can you come in for a minute? I want you to read something."

A HALF HOUR LATER, Colonel warms by the stone fireplace as I stroke his head. I usually feel self-conscious when someone reads my writing. It's so personal. At times it can feel like an invasion into my privacy. Whenever someone reads my writing, I'm opening myself up to judgement and rejection. But this time I feel somewhat numb. I can feel my spirit giving up, and it's like Seamus is my Hail Mary pass at the end of a close football game. Will it make it into the end zone, or will I come up a few yards too short?

Seamus closes my laptop with a gentle click—a stark contrast to my earlier reaction.

His pained expression is all I need to know how he feels. "He's right. I'm sorry, Kayleigh. Yer writing is grand, it really is, but it's missing heart."

Somehow, deep down, I knew he would confirm my fear. "I've lost it." I say it matter-of-factly, leaving no room for another opinion. "I lost my heart for writing."

Colonel nudges my leg.

"I may have lost my heart, but I found you, huh?" I rub his ears, and he rolls onto his back.

Seamus sits on the floor next to us. "Ya just need inspiration again. This story is structurally brilliant. The technical writing is grand."

"But the story isn't."

"The problem is that real life isn't perfect. It's as if ya were writin' from the outside, checkin' a box off a list, but not revealin' how ya feel about any of it."

"Like a robot."

He shrugs. "A wee bit in the writin'. There's more to ya than this. Ya have a writer's heart. It's what Professor Gaffney sees. It's what I see. Ya just need to let it show."

His words are like a sword twisting within me and a soothing balm at the same time. Somehow I knew I needed Seamus to help me see clearly.

"I think maybe I'm afraid to feel anything." And because of that, I sacrificed my writing.

"I think," Seamus says, looking into my eyes, "ya just need to find your inspiration again."

We're only inches apart when Colonel leaps from the rug in one fluid movement and runs to the window. The hair on his back rises, and a growl rumbles from his throat. Seamus follows him to the window, looking out into the dark night.

An engine rumbles before speeding down the drive, its head-lights a fading glare in the dense fog.

"Who was that?" I walk over next to Seamus.

"I can't say for sure, only whoever it was is not a friend."

Colonel stands next to me, a protectiveness in his posture. "Good boy, Colonel." I give him a kiss on the top of his head.

"Maybe it's a good thing he's here after all."

The sincerity in his voice has me wondering, not for the first time, if coming to Ireland was such a good idea.

THE NEXT MORNING, I'm sitting in the middle of a pew at St. Patrick's Catholic Church. Teagan is on my one side and Seamus on the other. Father Nolan stands in front of the congregation. He's tall and has a youthful demeanor with his dark curly hair and round face. His gentle smile is welcoming, and when he speaks, it's like listening to an old friend.

"We have a wonderful reminder in our second reading today." He gestures at the congregation with a friendly raise of his hand. "Jeremiah 29:11 tells us that God has a plan for our lives. His plan is one that brings fullness of life. He wants good for us, not harm. Jesus tells us that to be His disciple we must deny ourselves, take up our cross, and follow Him. Look at the apostles and the joy they radiate in doin' the work of the Lord. It doesn't mean they didn't have problems or obstacles. All of them were persecuted, and all but Saint John succumbed to martyrdom. Saint John is the unique one. He's the only apostle, along with Mother Mary and Mary Magdalene, mentioned at the Crucifixion. He followed the Lord's plan, even when that meant the potential for great harm and death. He was faithful to the very end."

He looks around the chapel, and his eyes catch mine for a brief moment. I quickly look away, and I'm not sure if it's because I know it's the truth, or I'm scared that if it's the truth I have failed so miserably lately.

"Ye may be sittin' here today, wonderin' what ye should do with yer life. Ya may even be asking yerself if yer life has any purpose at all."

There's a murmur among the congregation. I want to be a part of this community—a community that knows and understands each other so well. Berryville is my home, and the community could never be replaced, but there's something so very special about Cloverdale.

"I'm tellin' ye today that yer life has purpose. Ye are fearfully and wonderfully made." He pauses before continuing. "God is good, and all of His creation is good. That includes all of us, even me—although that may not always be evident, especially durin' our budget plannin' meetin's."

A light laughter rolls through the chapel. "God only creates good. There is bad in the world. Tragic things happen. Here in Cloverdale, we know this all too well. But, He can make even the most painful and tryin' times good. It's in those trials that we need to rely fully on God and see the light that He brings into our lives. The apostles followed God's plan for their lives, and despite the horrendous persecutions, they found joy in their situation because they allowed God to work in their lives. He is our strength when we're at our weakest. He's our sunlight in the storm."

He points to the crucifix hanging above the altar. "No matter the storm ye may be going through right now, trust in God's plan for ya, and ye will see the break in the clouds. The shimmer of light through the darkness. He will be yer guide, leading ye to the life ye were made to live."

"Right ya are," Nora says softly, taking Malachy's hand.

"Today," Fr. Nolan says, "I encourage ye to ask yerself— what is God's plan for my life? Listen to His answer. Then let go of yer own plans and follow His. I promise ye, His plan is better than anything we could ever imagine."

He turns around and walks behind the altar. The truth of his words is heavy on my heart.

What is God's plan for my life? I've considered my life many times, but I've never asked myself this particular question.

Could it be different from what I always imagined? And if it is, am I strong enough to surrender my will to His?

TWO DAYS LATER, I awaken to the sunlight streaming through my window. I immediately feel better with the warmth and understand now the significance of these days amidst all of the rain. I glance at my phone on the nightstand. A text message from Magnolia.

Getting on the plane now. I'll be there soon!

To say I'm excited to see Magnolia today is an understatement. I check the clock. She's due at the airport in three hours. We planned on just taking a taxi, but I have a better idea.

I text Seamus. *Any chance you could give me a ride to the airport?*

A moment later I receive his reply. *Yer not skipp'in the country, are ya?*

I laugh. *No. I have a friend visiting. Her flight gets in at noon."*

I'll pick ya up in an hour.

Seamus never hesitates to help anyone. *Thank you.*

I climb out of bed and begin getting ready. I slip on my long-sleeve white cotton dress with tiny blue forget-me-nots, matching blue leggings, and my white sneakers. I open the bedroom window, and a breeze flutters through, the earthy scent revitalizing me. It's about sixty-five degrees Fahrenheit and just the right amount of warmth on the breeze. I brush my long dark hair, the damp curls hanging midway down my back. I add a little black mascara and shiny pink lip gloss. I'm about to add a few swipes of pink blush to my cheeks, but they are already tinged from the fresh air. I close the blush compact and stash it into my cosmetic bag before adding thin gold hoops to my ears.

I tidy up the bedroom and then go into the kitchen to warm the tea kettle. I watch as the black breakfast tea seeps. I inhale the invigorating aroma while I fold the throw blankets on the sofa. Once everything is in order, I take my teacup out onto the swing in the front field. I swing gently back and forth watching the herring gulls flying over the bay. Their gray and white bodies speckle the sky, diving down occasionally like stunt pilots in a war movie. The damp ground under my feet gives off a mossy scent as the sun tries to dry up the remaining moisture.

I turn toward the driveway at the sound of crunching stones.

"There's Jemma," I tell Colonel.

He runs to the now parked car. His bark has turned into a happy whine, as his whole rear end shakes along with his tail. Seamus laughs and scratches Colonel's big head.

"Thanks for the ride, Seamus. I don't know what I'd do without you."

He kicks a stone from the drive like he's passing a soccer ball, and Colonel immediately chases after it. "Ya don't need to worry about that now."

I call Colonel into the cottage and give him a jerky treat while I wash the teacup and set it neatly on the hand towel. The set appears to be a family heirloom and used often over the years. The blue floral print has a few nicks and a chip in the porcelain, but it is a strong cup. There's no dishwasher in the cottage, and I imagine it being hand-washed many times over the years. I briefly wonder if it could have belonged to Seamus' mother. I wish I could've met his parents. Seamus is the sort of someone who makes you feel special, and I bet his parents were the same.

I lock the front door and meet Seamus at the car. He opens the passenger door for me, and I slide onto the worn leather seat.

"Uncle Malachy called while ya were in the cottage and asked if we could stop by the farm after the airport. There's somethin' important he wants to talk about. I know it's a lot to ask with yer friend here and all, but Aunt Nora's makin' dinner. Maybe yer friend would enjoy a visit? Teagan and Finn will be there too."

"I think she would love that." I think about the Kavanaghs and how much Magnolia would love to meet them. "What do you think Malachy wants to talk about?"

He starts the engine. "We can talk there."

What is Seamus not saying?

<hr>

"I CAN'T BELIEVE I'm actually here." Magnolia is as excited to see Brigid's Crossing and meet the Kavanaghs as I knew she would be. She actually seems in awe of everything so far, even as we waited for well over an hour to collect her suitcase, as it was accidentally sent to a different terminal.

"Ya first time in Ireland will do that to ya."

"I believe you're right about that." She stares out at the rolling hills, eyes round and intent on taking it all in.

"Hopefully this drizzle will stop soon," I say, noting that the dark clouds haven't changed much in the last hour.

"Oh, it just makes it more magical. The rain is like little diamonds."

"As long as it's not emeralds," Seamus jokes. I think everyone would be happy to never look for another stone after last year's treasure hunt.

I laugh. "So true."

"Oh, look at the sheep!" Magnolia puts a hand over her heart, seeming oblivious to us. "They're so precious."

Seamus' mouth tugs up on the side. "Aye. They make a good stew—"

"Look there's more!" I point towards the other side of the road, and Magnolia coos again.

Let her enjoy this, I mouth to Seamus.

"Americans," he mumbles, shaking his head.

Magnolia continues pointing out every sheep we pass on our way to the Kavanaghs, which is a lot more than I anticipated. Why didn't I ever notice? Was I so absorbed in my own troubles that I never noticed what surrounded me? Magnolia came to Ireland open to the experience. Sadly, I can't say the same for myself.

By the time we pull into the Kavanagh's drive, Seamus looks cautiously in the rearview mirror as we pass the Kavanaghs sheep on the far hill. I think he might go crazy if he hears any more about sheep. Luckily, Magnolia misses the sheep as she's intently staring at the farmhouse.

The old stone farmhouse stands picturesque in the center of the rolling green hills. The front door and window shutters are painted a bright yellow, creating a welcoming light on this dreary day. The shutters are shut over the windows, but a warm light glows from within.

"The front door is swinging with a bad hinge. We can go around back." Seamus opens a large black umbrella and walks around to my door. He opens the door and holds the umbrella over me as he does the same for Magnolia.

Magnolia and I huddle under the umbrella as we follow

Seamus around the side of the farmhouse, passing a small white cottage that I recognize as the one Finn stayed in during their summer research program. The rain is heavy now, pounding against the already soggy ground, splattering mud onto us. When we reach the back, there are various colors of muck boots scattered in front of the matching yellow rear door.

Seamus holds the door open for us, and we hurry inside and out of the rain. The Kavanaghs, Teagan, and Finn are sitting around the oval wooden kitchen table. Malachy Kavanagh is a grandfather figure to Teagan and our family. His ruddy complexion tells of long days outside. Bright, clear blue eyes and white hair peak out from under his brown tweed cap. He sits beside his wife, Nora, who is one of the strongest women I've ever met. Her shoulder-length grey-streaked blonde hair is full and vibrant, giving her fair round face a youthful glow. Deep laugh lines hug her dark blue eyes —eyes that are filled with wisdom and grit. The Kavanaghs embrace us in warm, jovial hugs, and I can see that Magnolia is already smitten with them.

"Where are Tommy and Antonella?" I ask, looking for the Kavanagh's farmhand and Diaz family relation that I met during my last visit. Nathair used Tommy to try to find the hidden emerald on the Kavanagh's farm. Antonella, the granddaughter of the Diaz daughter who shared a special friendship with Malachy during their time on the farm. Tommy was greatly injured in the process of trying to keep the Kavanagh's safe. "I haven't seen them yet."

"Oh, I can't believe I forgot to tell you." Teagan shakes her head. "Antonella went back to Columbia to help set up an equine-assisted therapy program in her hometown. She learned so much in our program and felt the calling to help bring equine-assisted therapy to those closest to her."

"That's amazing! And Tommy?"

Finn laughs. "He went with her to help on the farm."

"I'm not sure he can imagine a life without Antonella." Nora smiles.

"She still doesn't return his feelings?" I ask.

"Sadly, no."

"I'm sensing there's some kind of love story happening there?" Magnolia asks.

"Well," I say, "it's more that Tommy is madly in love with Antonella, but she only wants to be friends. So, whether it's a happily ever after or tragic love story is yet to be determined."

"Mmm. That's a hard one."

"Yeah," I agree, "but there's different kinds of love. I have to believe she loves him dearly as a friend. That's true love too."

Magnolia wraps her arm through mine. "It's the first time I've heard you talk about love since..."

Since Chris broke up with me.

"Well," I say, clearing my throat, "sometimes it's the end of a chapter, not the end of a story."

"So, you're open to love again?" Teagan asks, always getting right to the point.

I glance at Seamus, who's in a conversation with Finn and Malachy. "I think a good friend is a special kind of love too."

"And," Magnolia adds, "the best romantic loves begin with friendship. Just remember Maryanne and Colonel Brandon."

And suddenly, I see their relationship in a whole new light.

AN HOUR later we are in the sitting room having tea.

"I think it's time to discuss the note." Malachy places his wood bone China cup on its saucer.

"What note?" I ask.

"Seamus received a note," Teagan explains. "We're trying to figure out what to do about it."

What kind of note would cause this much apprehension?

A muscle in Seamus' jaw twitches. "A threat."

"A threat to you?" Why didn't he mention this earlier?

He averts his eyes from me. "They seem to have found my weakness."

Seamus is all strength. What could possibly be his weakness? And who are they anyway?

Frustration has me shifting on the sofa. "Can someone please explain what's going on?"

Malachy pulls a crumpled piece of paper from his jacket and hands it to Nora. She slides on her reading glasses and reads aloud. *"Next time it will be that pretty lass in the cottage."*

"I don't understand." Magnolia shakes her head.

I fill her in on the vandalism of Seamus' boat and the car at the cottage.

"We think whoever left the note is tryin' to get revenge." Malachy fiddles the cap now in his hands.

"Ryan. I'd bet my life on it." Seamus clenches his fists in his lap. "It has to be Nathair."

"Revenge for what?" Magnolia asks, and I remember I may not have filled her in on all of the finer details about what happened last year.

"Because we beat Ryan to the emerald, and his girlfriend is in prison," Teagan says matter-of-factly. "Ryan is heavily embedded in the Nathair gang and posed as a friend to Seamus, working with him on his fishing boat and at the pub."

"But, if he is trying to get revenge for the emerald and

Fiona, then why go after Seamus? Why not come back to the farm?" I ask.

"Seamus is a way for Ryan and Nathair to get to Malachy and Nora," Finn explains.

"See, Nora and I never had any children of our own," Malachy says, squeezing Nora's hand. "And Seamus is as close as a son could be. And he is our heir."

"We are helping to fund *Rocky Shore Fishin'*," Nora continues, "and if the business is in danger, then they can try to use it against us."

Even with the short time that I've known the Kavanaghs, I know that they would help anyone in need. They would never let Seamus suffer if they could help it. If I understand that, then Ryan and Nathair must too.

"I won't let 'em!" Seamus stands and begins pacing back and forth in front of the stone fireplace. His loyalty to his family is evident with each word. "If I ever get my hands on—"

"Now, now," Nora soothes, "we've never backed down from a fight and don't intend to now. This is our land, our family, and our town, and we'll do everythin' we can to protect what we love."

"Right ya are," Malachy agrees. "Seamus don't go riskin' yer business for this. We will find a way to end it."

Their unity is inspiring, but I'm not sure how they plan to do so.

"Garda Connell has been filled in on everything, and they have a few leads," Finn says.

"We pray they will find out who's behind this soon." Nora takes a sip from her tea.

'Could it be the men from the market?' I ask, thinking of the confrontation with the mayor.

"Unfortunately not." Malachy looks to the floor. "They are just the middlemen."

Seamus runs a frustrated hand through his hair. "The problem is no one knows exactly who's in the gang."

There's a weighted silence before the door creaks open. A thin woman with a brown pixie cut and watery brown eyes stands in the doorway. Her lip trembles as she takes a step into the room.

"I do."

CHAPTER SIX

"My uncle Michael O'Doherty was part owner of *O'Doherty and Brannan's Pot o' Gold*." The woman sends a tepid glance to Malachy and Nora.

Malachy rubs his left temple with his thumb.

"Oh, dear." Nora pulls her rosary from her apron pocket. Her fingers begin moving along the beads.

"Wait." Teagan turns to Nora. "The same O'Doherty from the tale?"

"I'm afraid so." She rocks back and forth.

"What tale?" I ask.

"Well," Teagan says, narrowing her eyes at the woman, who I now understand is Caitlin O'Doherty, "I think it's Caitlin's story to tell."

Caitlin colors at Teagan's glare. "I never wanted to be a part of this."

"But, it looks like you are, so why don't you tell us the story." Finn's anger seems to radiate from him. He and Teagan have said nothing but good things about Caitlin and her equine-assisted therapy center. This is a blow to everything they thought they knew.

When Caitlin silently wipes her tears without responding, Nora speaks up instead. "Malachy's cousin, James Brannan, and his best mate, Michael, spent their childhood days inseparable. Runnin' the streets and playin' football in a wee village in County Donegal. They grew up into fine young fellas and started fishin' together in the Donegal Bay. They were top o' the line fishermen. Brought in flounder, mackerel, pollack, codlin', sea trout, and dogfish by the bucketful. They were a great team." She smiles at the memory.

"One day," Nora continues, "Michael's sister joined 'em. Erin was not much older than ten or eleven with long golden hair and bright blue eyes. As blue as the Connemara water, they say. She was the apple of Michael's eye, and a finer older brother there never was. Erin had been on the boat with them many times before, but that day a storm was brewin' off the coast."

Seamus shifts uncomfortably next to me on the sofa, memories of his own parents no doubt on his mind.

"The roughest storm in ages came upon the bay that day," Malachy says, leaning his elbows on his knees and picking up where Nora left off. "Many a business was ruined and never to be seen again. Never seen anything like it in the town."

"Did they survive the storm?" I ask.

"All three of 'em went overboard, the waves pushin' 'em under o'er and o'er again. They were grand swimmers, like all the townspeople, but it was no match for the strength of those waves. They knew they couldn't make it back to shore." He pauses, letting this sink in.

At our expectant faces, he continues. "They prayed for a miracle. It was their only hope left. No sooner did the words leave their mouths that a broken piece of wood from their ship floated right past them. Uncle James grabbed it, and they were able to paddle toward shore."

"That's right," Nora pats Malachy's knee. "And just as they

were closin' in on the shore, a rogue wave slammed into 'em—pullin' wee Erin into the water while pushin' the lads to the shore. The wave caused Michael to hit his head on a broken plank, and he was bleedin', in and out of consciousness laying on the shore. James ran back into the bay toward Erin's bobbin' head, but another wave crashed, and he could no longer see her."

"But, good ol' Uncle James," Malachy says, "sent another prayer up to the heavens, and the rain and wind ceased. The sun shined onto the water, just above where Erin was submerged. He dove under the miraculously calm water and pulled the lassie out. Then, he swam back to the shore, bringin' Erin right along with him."

I picture the rough sea and the suddenly calm water. What must that have been like to witness? To know that by the grace of God, you're given another chance at life.

"They swore," Caitlin says, voice quiet, "that it was their faith that saved Erin that day."

"That's right." Malachy studies Caitlin. "That faith led to a deep friendship, as deep as only friendships founded on faith can be."

"When Michael awoke," Nora continues, "and learned what James had done, he promised to repay him one day. And a couple years later when he bought an empty shop on Main Street, they opened *O'Doherty and Brannan's Pot o' Gold* together."

"The luckiest jewelry store in Ireland." Caitlin recites their tagline.

"They were partners?" Magnolia asks. "It must have been wonderful to go into business with your best friend."

I wonder if she misses the cafe at home now that she's in Ireland and so far away from it. So much of herself was put into creating Magnolia's Cafe.

"They were a grand team." Nora nods. "But, the store was sold years ago."

"Why? It sounds like they had a good thing going," I ask.

"They did," Malachy says, "but there was a feud that started between the two. In the end, it broke them. Neither was ever the same again."

"What was the feud about?" I ask, unwilling to allow the idea of a true friendship breaking apart so easily. "There must've been a way to repair it."

"Not everything can be repaired," Caitlin says. "Not when a person changes and is no longer himself anymore."

"When a man's soul is crushed, that's when you really need a miracle. And unfortunately for them, a miracle didn't come in time."

"Well, are they still around?" I scour my mind for a way to make things right. "If they are, it's still possible."

"Neither are with us anymore." Nora slides her rosary back into her pocket. "Their time has passed."

"So," Teagan says, looking at Caitlin, "why did you call us in the first place? I no longer believe it was just to work together."

Caitlin fidgets with her necklace before looking Teagan in the eye. "I was contacted by a man who said if I didn't help, he would ruin my farm. My program would end, and everything I ever dreamed of would be lost."

"Help you do what?" Finn asks.

Caitlin looks around at each of us. "I was told to get close to Teagan and Finn through *Second Chances* and provide an inside connection to the Kavanaghs and the farm."

"But, why?" I ask, still so confused about her role in all of this.

"I don't know much, except that he believes the Kavanaghs owe him for a past offense."

"Who was the man who called you?" Seamus' eyes are cold. "Is he a part of Nathair?

"I don't know his name. All I know is that he works at Emerald Isle."

COLONEL'S big wet nose nudges me awake the next morning. Through groggy eyes I see him wagging his tail, ready to go outside. He gives a whine, and I roll over, covering my head with the pillow. Maybe he will just go back to sleep.

Wishful thinking.

He hops up on top of me, causing the bed frame to creak threateningly.

"Okay, you win!" I push him off, and he whines in delight.

I step into my fluffy baby blue slippers and slide into my matching blue robe. Strands of hair hang loosely from the braid slung over my shoulder.

I clip his leash to his collar, knowing very well that if he wanted he could pull away and run. I open the front door, and a folded Cloverdale Herald newspaper lays on the blue welcome mat. The local newspaper is packed full of Cloverdale news, in-depth political and entertainment stories, event coverage, and personal essays. I always enjoy the weekly prints and find myself looking forward to reading the stories each week. I normally read the newspaper at the university library though. There's never been one on my doorstep before.

I bend down to pick it up, but Colonel pulls hard on the leash. "Okay, okay. Let's go for a walk first."

Colonel smells every tree, bush, and flower along the way. He barks at three seagulls flying overhead and chases a rabbit over one too many hills, with me screeching behind. By the time we make it back to the cottage, I've almost forgotten about the newspaper.

I unclip Colonel's leash and let him in the cottage. He runs to his water bowl and drinks all the contents. I use this quiet time to retrieve the newspaper, immediately noticing the tagged page.

Kayleigh, maybe you'll find inspiration here. The note is written in black ink and what I'm quickly learning is Seamus' handwriting. I look at the employment advertisement he circled.

Writer Wanted
Personal Essay Assignment
Topics are negotiable but must be relevant
to the Cloverdale community
Apply via the email address below

"What's that?"

I turn to find Magnolia walking out of the guest bedroom in her pink and white flower pajamas. "A job listing for a writer for the Cloverdale Herald."

"That's interesting. Are you looking for a job?"

Before seeing this advertisement, I would have said no, but there's something about the job that interests me.

"Not really." I read the listing again. "I can't put my finger on why, but it feels like I should apply. Is that weird?"

"Not weird, but interesting that you feel this way. Where did you find the paper?"

"Seamus left it at the front door. He circled it for me." I show her the listing.

"Well, I see why you feel this way now." She grins at me.

"I know that look." I point at her. "It's not because of Seamus."

"Okay, if you say so." She doesn't look convinced.

Instead of arguing the point, I consider the listing again. "It's an opportunity to get to know the community better and write for fun again."

Magnolia's teasing smile disappears. "Is writing not fun anymore?"

"Not really." As soon as the words are out I know they're true. It's something that I've felt within me the past weeks, but hearing myself say it out loud confirms my fear. Writing is no longer fun.

"I'm so sorry to hear that. I love your stories. Do you think it's the stress of university?"

"Somewhat." I think back to Professor Gaffney's evaluation of my writing. "I feel lost in my writing. Like, I can still write, but something's missing."

"Inspiration."

How does everyone but me seem to see this so clearly?

"That's what Seamus said too."

"Oh, really. Well, that makes me like him all the more now."

"If it's just because I lack inspiration, how do I find it?"

Magnolia holds up the paper. "Maybe Seamus is on to something here. Maybe this job will help you to find inspiration again."

Could this job hold the key to finding inspiration? A part of me wants to refute this thought, push it aside as another thing that will leave me empty in the end. But another part, a part growing bigger by the second, believes her words. There's something here. Whether it's just a reporter's intuition or a writer's hope, it's there.

I turn on my laptop and click on the mailbox. "What's the email?"

I type out a quick response to the listing and send it with an unspoken prayer in my heart. I stash the newspaper between my schoolbooks on the kitchen table. We grab a couple of orange scones from the bakery box and venture out for a walk down to the dock.

After spending an hour on the dock, catching up on news from home, we come back to the cottage invigorated by the salty air and companionship. When I open my laptop to work on my history assignment, there's a new message waiting for me in my inbox.

Dear Kayleigh,

Thank you for inquiring about the reporter position. Your message and CV are impressive, and we would like to set up an interview in two weeks. Details are included in the attachment. Please bring your portfolio with writing samples and an article proposal for the interview. The proposal should be a personal essay of interest in the Cloverdale community.

We look forward to seeing you soon.

Thank you,
Patrick Dempsey
Editor in Chief

"I got an interview."

Magnolia takes an apple from the ceramic fruit bowl on the kitchen counter and joins me at the table. "Of course you did. You deserve it."

"I meet with the editor in two weeks, and I need to bring writing samples and an article proposal—a personal essay on a topic relevant to Cloverdale."

"Well, you have lots of great articles you've written. Those will show how great a reporter and writer you are." She beams at me. "Start with those and see if they inspire a new idea. I think this may be where you find your inspiration."

"I'll find inspiration in the story?"

"Perhaps. Or in the process of writing the story. I think there's something here for you. You're always writing other people's stories; maybe it's time to write your own."

My own story. The idea is exciting and frightening at the same time.

"Where would I even begin?"

She gestures to me. "I think you've already begun. Look at yourself. There's something different about you."

There is something different about me. I can feel it too. It's like something I was holding back, overshadowed for so long, is bursting to come out.

A text message alerts on my phone. *I saw the listing and thought of you.*

Magnolia glances at the screen. "He really cares about you."

I swipe the phone off and lay it back on the table. "Seamus is just a good guy. He likes helping people. Knight complex and all that."

"I don't know. I think it's more than that. I can see it in the way he looks at you."

Her words send my heart pounding. Haven't I felt it when he looks at me? When our eyes connect, there's something there. "What if he does care for me, as you say?"

Magnolia places her apple aside. "Then, it just depends on how you feel."

"What if I don't know how I feel?" Or what if I want to deny how I feel?

"That's okay too."

And for now, it has to be okay.

THE NEXT MORNING I take the trolley into Dublin while Magnolia stays at the cottage. I'm meeting Professor Gaffney at the Emerald Isle library after my morning classes. He didn't say why he wants to meet, and after my latest writing critique, my nerves are on edge.

As I pull open the heavy wooden door, the scent of old books flows through the air. The odor invigorates me as though thousands of past writers are providing support. I step through the doorway and scan the sitting area for Professor Gaffney. I spot the gray tweed cap and his reddish blond hair sticking out of the brim.

"Hi, Professor."

"Kayleigh." He smiles, and his green eyes twinkle behind his round golden glasses. "Thanks for meetin' with me."

I shake his extended hand and sit in the brown leather chair opposite him. There's a scattered collection of British literature texts on the table between us and a large stack of papers. An old yellow porcelain teacup sits on a matching saucer.

"I have a wee bit o' papers to grade." He chuckles. "The reason I asked you here today is because I see a lot of promise in your writin'."

This throws me off as his critique is heavy on my mind. If I have so much promise, why did he have so much to say that denies this?

When I don't say anything, he gives another chuckle. "What I'm sayin' is that I'd like to mentor you—help you grow in your writin'. That is, if you'd like me as a mentor. I can be a bit harsh at times, but it's all to help you write in a way that I know you can."

I am shell-shocked by his offer but know that I have to say something instead of just sitting here dumbfounded. My conversation with Samara comes to mind. "You want me to be in Gaffney's Guild?"

"Ah, do the students still call it that?" He shakes his head. "I am always fascinated by the workin's of gifted minds. I must confess, there is no group or club. That is a figment of folklore. Though, I have chosen students from my courses who stand out in ability and mentor them in their personal writing technique beyond the classroom. I push them to sharpen their skills and hopefully lead them to publishin'."

"I would love to have my writing published one day."

He considers me for a moment. "I believe if ya work through this barrier ya're up against, then there's no doubt we will all be seein' your books in the future."

What would it feel like to hold my own book in my hands? I try to picture it. I feel the rush of excitement but pause at the blank book cover. What will my story be?

"But," he cautions, "remember my words. If ya're not writtin' from the heart, we'll all miss out on yer words."

The image of myself as a published writer slips away.

"So," he says brightly, "are you currently workin' on anythin' besides my assignments, of course?"

I shake myself out of the daze. "Actually, yes. I'm about to write a news article."

A thin line furrows between his eyebrows. "I didn't realize ya're a member of the paper."

"Not the university one," I say, a little too quickly. "I applied for a position with the Cloverdale Herald. I have an interview coming up but need to bring an article proposal. If the interview goes well, and the editor likes my writing and the proposal, then I'll not only have the job and great experience for my resume, but my story will be printed in the paper."

"I see." He nods and brings his pen to his lips in concentration. "And what story ideas are ya floatin' around?"

"*O'Doherty and Brannan's Pot o' Gold.*" The idea comes without hesitation. "I heard about how the owners were best friends, and then everything just fell apart. It's so sad. I don't know the whole story, not yet, but it's one that I want to learn more about. I think it will be fascinating to write a piece on it. I plan to look for some old newspaper articles about the store while I'm here today."

"Well, research is the key to good reportin'." He picks up his teacup and takes a sip. "Key to good novel writin' as well. The story must feel real. The reader needs to feel like they're in the settin', the authenticity of the characters and dialogue flowin' 'round 'em. The plot should be natural and gripping. Do you think this story will grip readers?"

I consider how I felt when I first learned about the story. "Yes," I say confidently. "I really do."

And I spend the next half hour telling him all that I know of O'Doherty and Brannon and their Pot o' Gold.

A COUPLE OF HOURS LATER, I am immersed in the newspaper clippings and history books. In all of the information about the store, I haven't found a single reason or even a suggestion for the feud. The feud is where the story lies. I just need to uncover it.

"Still workin' I see." Professor Gaffney stands by my table, stack of papers in his hands and leather briefcase slung over his shoulder.

I sigh. "Yes. I'm having a bit of trouble with one part."

"Which part?"

"The plot." I heave a deep sigh. I can hear Ashling telling me not to be overdramatic.

He raises his eyebrows. "The plot. Well, that's a pretty big part."

I laugh. "It sure is, and unfortunately, I'm no closer than I was when I started. I've only found the parts of the story that

I already know, but what I want to know is what caused the feud that closed the store. I mean, it would have had to be a big deal to close something so important to the both of them. And to destroy a friendship like theirs."

"I believe ya're right." He shrugs. "In my experience there's only one thing that has gotten between my mates to end a friendship."

I sit up straighter in the chair. "What's that?"

"A lass."

Why hadn't I thought of this? "Of course."

"I don't know about them, but it has been known to happen."

"That makes sense. Now, I just need to find a way discover if it's true."

"I've always thought that the best research is done on the ground. And I think you will find a way."

He gives a brief nod before walking out the library doors, leaving me with my first real lead to go on since beginning my research.

He's right—the best research is done on the ground. I need to visit the shop. Somehow I know that's where the story lies.

I PUSH thoughts of visiting the old shop to the back of my mind as Magnolia and I get ready for tonight's ceilidh at Lockhaven Castle.

"Alright, which shoes?" Magnolia holds up one white sneaker and one caramel brown leather ankle boot.

"My heart is saying the boots, but I can hear Teagan saying the sneakers are more practical and would be more comfortable."

Magnolia scrunches her nose looking between the two. "So, the boots?"

"Absolutely." I hold up my own soft white leather ankle boots to match hers.

We laugh as she hugs the boot to her chest. "We'll just wear our comfiest socks. That should be good."

"Agreed." I choose white ankle socks with a little more padding than the sheer ones. I slide my feet into the boots and check my reflection in the full-length gold rimmed mirror. My long-sleeved white tunic shirt is one of my favorites and flows over my rose-colored leggings. My long dark hair is hanging down my back, loose curls are pulled back from the sides in a twist held by a gold clip. I swipe a touch of pink blush to my cheeks and apply matching lip gloss. I line my eyes with a soft navy color and highlight the lids with a shimmery pink, adding a slightly deep rose color to the outer corners. A few strokes of navy mascara bring the blue of my eyes out without being too much.

"Let's see how long these curls last in the rain." Magnolia turns her curling iron in a circle before releasing a light blonde tendril. Her shoulder-length hair is curled in sections giving it a dimensional appearance. She's wearing straight-leg indigo jeans and a white and blue toile printed button-down top. The top is tied in a cute knot on her hip, and her gold and white enamel magnolia flower necklace lays just above her collarbone. Black eyeliner and moody silver shadow highlights her gray eyes. Peach blush and matching lips give her a girl-next-door-with-an-edge vibe.

Colonel gives a few happy yelps by the front door.

"Seamus must be here," I tell Magnolia before walking to the front door.

Colonel's back end is shaking back and forth with obvious excitement, and I don't blame him—I'm feeling the same way.

When I open the door, Seamus is standing on the welcome mat with two small bouquets of roses, one yellow and the other red. The rain has slowed to a mist sparkling in the lantern by the door. Little beads of water cling to his black hair, and I have the urge to brush the damp strands from his forehead.

"Hi, Kayleigh." His deep Irish lilt hits me straight in the heart.

"Hi." I can't seem to pull my eyes from him.

"Can I come in?" he asks, amusement in his voice.

"Of course!" I step aside, and he walks into the cottage. I close the door firmly behind him to keep the dampness out.

"Oh, you brought flowers!" Magnolia joins us with a big smile.

"Aye, can't go to a ceilidh without a flower or two." He glances at me, and there's something unspoken in his eyes.

"These are for you." He does an exaggerated bow and hands Magnolia the yellow roses.

"Why thank you!" She curtsies back and sends me a look that says, 'Come on, look at him.'

He takes a couple of steps so that he's right in front of me. He reaches for my hand and draws it up to his lips. "My lady."

My hand tingles from his kiss as I take the bouquet of red roses. "Thank you. They're beautiful."

"I could say the same about you." His eyes linger on mine.

Not liking anyone too close to me, Colonial jumps up on him, knocking him into the antique wrought iron floor lamp. They both crash to the floor, the sound of metal snapping.

"No!" I reach out to catch the stained glass lamp shade, but I'm just out of reach, and it hits the floor hard.

Tiny pieces of yellow and green glass scatter across the hardwood floor as Magnolia gasps.

"Seamus, are you okay?" I lean down next to him.

"I told ya that dog is a nuisance." He rubs Colonel's big head, checking him for any injuries.

"I don't think there's any way to save the lamp." Magnolia grimaces.

We look at the shattered pieces of stained glass covering the floor.

"I'm so sorry, Seamus. It must have been a family heirloom." I fiddle with a rose in an attempt to release my nervous energy.

He examines a few pieces of glass. "I'll find a way to mend it, and it will be as good as new."

"I'll help you fix it. There has to be a way to mold the glass back together."

Seamus gives me a kind smile. "I'm sure there is."

Magnolia takes the bouquet of roses out of my hands. "I'll find vases for the roses."

She shuffles around the kitchen cabinets as Seamus and I clean up the pieces of glass. Colonel looks rightfully abashed and is watching us from his spot in front of the fireplace.

"I found vases!" Magnolia calls.

"That's not a vase," I say as she carries a large glass bowl into the sitting room.

"I found this *next* to the vases."

I run my finger over the edging. The rim is intricately carved in a wave pattern, resembling the sea. "It's incredible."

The bowl is studier than I expected at first glance. The detail creates a three-dimensional feel when the light hits it, giving the appearance of moving water.

"It's Waterford crystal." Seamus joins us. "I haven't seen this in a long time."

Magnolia carefully hands Seamus the bowl.

He looks at the bowl with a mixture of sadness and joy. "Da had this made for their tenth wedding anniversary. He worked with a designer in Waterford. I remember the day he brought it home. Ma was making her pot roast—the one Da loved so much. He walked through that door, a wide grin on his face. The bowl was wrapped in one of his wool fisherman's sweaters. When he lifted the sleeves and Ma saw the bowl, she gasped and dropped the roast onto the floor." He laughs at the memory. "She gushed over that bowl like it was the prized jewel of the royal kingdom. She told him it was too much, and they didn't have the funds, but he said nothin' was too much for her. That the bowl would always remind them of their love and their home by the sea."

"Oh." Magnolia covers her mouth with her hand. "That is so precious."

Seamus' eyes glisten. "Da had the heart of a poet."

Just like Seamus.

"Should I put it back in the cabinet?" Magnolia asks, glancing at the broken glass still on the floor.

"No." Seamus shakes his head. "It should be out for all to see. I never should have hidden it in the first place."

"I have an idea." I bend down and pick up a handful of glass. I gently place the pieces in the bowl. The reflection of the colors and the crystal creates a sparking rainbow. "Maybe we can keep the glass in here, just until we can get it repaired."

"Oooh, I love it!" Magnolia gushes.

I look to Seamus, and he nods. We collect the rest of the glass pieces from the floor and fill the bowl. Putting them together in the crystal bowl is like giving them new life.

"Ma and Da would've loved this." Seamus runs a hand along my back. "We better get to the ceilidh before the dancin' is over."

And I walk out the front door with my best friend and the guy who just may be mending the pieces of my own heart.

CHAPTER SEVEN

The rhythmic music of a jig welcomes us as we enter through the large heavy doors of Lockhaven Castle. The medieval hall is packed with townspeople swinging in choreographed circles around the dance floor. A half dozen long rectangular tables filled with food and drink line the perimeter bursting with hearty conversation.

"This is amazing," Magnolia says as laughter rings out from the dance floor.

The townspeople are lining up in two lines. They move in a natural procession from years of practice. We find an empty spot at a table along the far side wall.

"Hey!" Teagan places her pint on the table as Finn hands her a basket of Reuben egg rolls. "These are delicious." She holds the basket out to us.

Magnolia samples an egg roll. "Wow, they really are. I love the dressing."

Seamus takes a large bite of his. "They're packed with corned beef, the finest aged sauerkraut, and local melted cheese. The dressing is Ms. O'Grady's secret though. I've been pressin' her for years, but no luck yet."

"I think I need to speak with this Ms. O'Grady." Magnolia glances around the hall. "Is she here tonight?"

Seamus points to the opposite side of the room. "She's right o'er there. Short gray hair and green jumper. Best of luck to ya."

"I'll be back—and with the special ingredient." Magnolia winks at us before crossing the room.

"She's a determined one."

I watch Magnolia introduce herself to Ms. O'Grady. "She has to be to run the cafe like she does at home."

"I'd like to go there sometime."

I'm caught off guard by his comment. "Where? America?"

"Aye. Yer Berryville sounds like a grand place to visit."

Excitement bubbles within me at the thought of Seamus in my hometown. "Well, if you're ever in the area, I'll show you myself."

He finishes off the Reuben egg roll. "Now I'm sold. I'll buy my ticket tomorrow."

I laugh. "I never thought you'd want to go to America. Seems you're right at home here."

"I could never leave Cloverdale—for good that is. But, I wouldn't mind travelin' a bit. I went straight to work after secondary and never ventured out like my lads."

Seamus has done so much with his life. His fishing business alone is a huge accomplishment at such a young age, just like Magnolia with the cafe. I've never considered either of them having regrets about things they didn't do. I see their accomplishments and then forget all that they must have given up achieving them. Now, I wonder what other dreams Seamus pushed aside to get to where he is.

"Maybe you can still find a way to do some traveling sometime. I know I'd love to visit Venice one day."

He raises an eyebrow. "Venice? The city of love."

My cheeks warm. "Yeah. Venice has a lot of history—traditional, you know? It's not because it's the city of love."

"Right." He sounds anything but convinced. "History."

"So, what's this dance?" I ask to change the subject.

"The Haymaker's Jig. An old favorite. It has a lot of history and it's tradition, ya know." He draws out the last part, emphasizing each word.

I turn away to hide my smile. "Well, history and tradition are very important."

"Ya won't hear an argument from me."

We watch as the couples line up in two rows.

Seamus holds a hand out to me. "Care to make a little tradition of our own?"

I take his hand. "I can't turn down a chance for that, now can I?"

He leads me to one of the rows. When he starts to walk to the other, I grab his hand.

"Where are you going? Don't leave me. I have no idea what I'm doing."

"Relax. It's an easy one. As yer partner, I stand across from ya."

I don't let go of his hand. He gives me a curious look before bringing my hand up to his lips and brushing the top with a light kiss. "Believe me, Kayleigh. I would never leave ya."

My hand still tingles as I watch him walk to the other side, his absence felt more than I would like. James Kenny, the old postal in a white button-down dress shirt and brown slacks, speaks about the rise and grind jig step and swinging our partners.

"Ya promenade in and out two times, jig step, and then repeat. The top gent and the bottom lady go 'round by right hands and the other side follows. Then, you repeat it. The next part has been known to throw a man's back out." He waits as the group laughs among themselves. "But, we'll have none of that tonight, right Malachy?"

"Ah, go on with ya! Stop yer gabbing, and I'll show ya how it's done." Malachy, face flushed, points a finger at James.

"Jesus, Mary, and Joseph," Nora murmurs, "please not this again." She crosses herself.

"Take it easy Malachy, ya're not as young as ya once were.'" James continues with an ornery curve of his mouth.

"I outta—"

"As I was sayin, the top gent and the bottom lady will meet in the middle and swing for sixteen beats. After, they take right hands and go 'round half turns with their partner to take the left hands of the opposite line and turn with the line. The couple will meet at the top and then swing down the center of the lines for sixteen beats, ending back in the middle for another swing. The tops lead their lines around to the end where the couple makes an arch for the remaining couples to cross under, leaving us with a new top and bottom couple."

All the talk of swinging already has my head spinning. The people around me are all nodding like what he just said makes sense when I'm more confused than ever. I glance at Teagan and Finn, who are second in line. Teagan appears to be mumbling the directions over again, using her hands to repeat the sequence.

My apprehension must show because the empathetic lady next to me pats my back. "Just follow his lead, lass, and it'll be just fine."

All I can manage is a smile before the upbeat music begins. The first couple skillfully dances around. The first time the middle-aged gent reaches me, he leads me in the half turn with ease and gentleness. "You're doin' grand," he tells me before moving on down the line.

His kindness does the trick, reminding me that this is supposed to be fun. It doesn't matter that I don't know what I'm doing because Seamus does. As he leads me through the arch, I know I can trust him.

Teagan and Finn start their turn by missing each other's hands. After trying again, they turn the wrong way ending on opposite lines. James calls out the steps, but they can't seem to be on the same time for any of it.

"Teagan, dear," Nora calls over the music, "just follow Finn's lead."

The look Teagan shoots her has me biting my lip to keep from laughing. I look away from the mess of their steps and meet Seamus' eyes. Laughter shines in them, and I know he's feeling the same as me. It's a nice feeling to you can say so much with just a look.

By the time it's our turn, we've gone through the sequence so many times that my nerves have relaxed, and we glide together seamlessly. I find myself counting the beats until I get to meet Seamus again. His hand takes mine, and our movements are so intertwined that I don't even think of the steps.

As I spin around and around, the crowd blurs into the background, the music is a distant echo, and all I can see is Seamus. When we finally stop, I feel off-balance, but whether it's from the dance or Seamus I'm not sure.

"It was like watching Emma and Mr. Knightly dancing at the ball." Magnolia is at my side. "You two are the perfect couple."

The last time I over-romanticized a Jane Austen relationship I ended up blind to reality and left heartbroken. It's not something I want to repeat. I watch as Seamus helps Malachy, who's hunched over and holding his back, to the table. Nora is waving her finger at Malachy.

"So," I say, redirecting the conversation, "did you get the secret ingredient?"

She beams at me. "I sure did!"

I listen as Magnolia talks about how she can't wait to use the recipe when she returns home, and I try not to imagine Seamus visiting or the way his eyes capture my heart.

———

A WEEK LATER, I wake up to a quiet cottage. Colonel is still snoring at the foot of my bed, but there's no footsteps in the hall or laughing in the breakfast nook. Magnolia left for home last night, and I already miss her. It was so nice having her visit, but as she said, the cafe was waiting for her at home. I roll over, hugging my pillow close, and close my eyes. My alarm sounds just as I'm falling back to sleep, and I hit the snooze. It's Saturday, why did I set my alarm anyway?

The interview.

I jump up, hitting my elbow on the headboard. "Ouch!"

I have my interview at the Cloverdale Herald in an hour, and I almost just slept right through it. I hurry into the bathroom, but when there's a scratch at the door I remember that Colonel needs to go outside.

"Alright, let's go," I tell him, grabbing my rain jacket and pulling on my wellies. I don't bother changing out of my pajamas since I know we'll only be out for a few minutes. I open the front door, and the rain is coming down harder than I expected.

"Wait, Colonel, we need the umbrella." I step back inside and grab the large black umbrella from the coat rack.

As I shut the door, Colonel strains against his leash. "Okay, okay. I'm coming."

As we come back from around the side of the cottage Colonel stops. A low growl vibrates from deep within his throat. The rain pounds against the umbrella, and water runs down my bare legs. I follow his gaze towards the bay.

A man stands on the dock, dressed all in black. His rain slicker reaches down to his knees, and the hood is pulled up over his head, obstructing any view of his face. He wears black sunglasses despite the heavy rain. Goosebumps prickle my skin.

"Let's go inside." My voice shakes as I give Colonel another tug on the leash.

He backs up slowly towards the door. I grab the doorknob and turn, but it doesn't budge. Could I have locked the door?

No. I never lock the door when I take Colonel out. *The wood warps in the rain.* Seamus' words come back to me. He warned me that this happens. The moisture expands the wood, and it jams in the door frame. Colonel growls louder this time, his sharp teeth peeking out from under his twitching lips. Fear grips my heart as I expect the man to come closer, but he continues to stand there. I force myself to look right back. After a few moments, he climbs onto the jet ski bobbing next to the dock and takes off over the choppy water, his dark figure fading into the bay.

I use my body and push against the door as hard as I can. There's a creaking in the wood before it pops open. I slip inside, Colonel at my heels, and lock the door. I stand with my back against the door for a few moments as I try to steady my heartbeat. Colonel peers through the window, ears alert.

Who was that man?

There was nothing familiar about him. His attire points to Nathair. But, what was he doing here?

"Next time it will be that pretty lass in the cottage."

An image of the crumpled note flashes in my mind. They are following through with their threat. The realization doesn't stir the fear and anxiety I expect, but rather anger. How dare they use me to get to Seamus and the Kavanaghs.

All of my life people have brushed me aside thinking I'm this delicate flower unable to cope with the real world. Even Teagan and Ashling treat me like someone who needs protecting and sheltering. They think I live in these fantasies in my mind. Seamus in his knight regalia flashes through my mind. I don't want to be the princess who always needs saving. For once, I want to be the one who saves myself.

I step away from the door and feel stronger than I did before. Colonel lays in his spot in front of the hearth, providing assurance that we are safe now.

Regardless of what just happened, it's time to get ready for the interview.

"Ms. Kayleigh O'Reilly?" A petite girl, who looks to be around my age, calls from the doorway of the small lobby. She holds a clipboard in her one hand as she smooths her chin-length jet black hair with her other. Large red feathers dangle from her ears, matching her red and orange swing dress.

"I'm Kayleigh," I say as I walk towards her. My portfolio holding my article proposal and writing samples are tucked neatly in the leather bag.

When I wrote the article proposal earlier this week, I tried to image what it was like for Michael O'Doherty and James Brannan to open their store. Magnolia and I have talked for years about expanding the cafe to include a book nook. She would manage the restaurant portion, and I would run the book area. It would be the perfect balance of comfort and rest. Currently, Magnolia lives in the loft apartment over the cafe, but when she has a family, she says she would love to live in one of the town's many old farmhouses, and it would leave the loft open for the book nook. The wooden beams, wall of built-in bookcases, and brick accent wall with a wood-burning fireplace invites long hours of rest and reading. It is easy to imagine how it would feel to work with your best friend. It was harder to comprehend how the rift between the friends happened. Professor Gaffney shined light on the possibility of a woman being the cause. As of now, it's the best lead I have, but there's no evidence a woman even existed.

"I'm Fiadh." She pronounces her name Fee-ah.

"I love your name. It's beautiful."

"Ya're too kind. It means wild—at least that's what Da always says. Tells me no name would suit me better. Although, Ma says it also means deer and respect, so I'm not sure which to actually go with. Although, I think Da may be the winner."

I laugh, immediately liking her and her open spirit. "Well, my name means a woodland meadow. I'm not sure if it is like me at all."

"I can see it. Ya have a peaceful grace about yerself. I looked over yer file—it's my job," she assures me, "and I knew there was somethin' special about ya."

"Thank you," I tell her, feeling a boost in my confidence. "I hope I get the job."

"It won't be easy, since ya're the youngest applicant and have the least experience."

My confidence falters as quickly as it came.

It must show in my expression because she covers her mouth with her hand. "I'm terribly sorry. I didn't mean it like that."

I wave her off. "No worries, I understand."

"Da just always follows the rules and goes with what looks best on paper. But, I think it'll be different with ya."

"Oh, is Mr. Dempsey–"

"My da? He is."

We stop outside an office door, and she leans into me. "He has a good heart. He'll see ya're the right choice."

She knocks twice on the door before opening it and waving me in. "Best of luck, Kayleigh. I hope to be working together soon." She sends me an encouraging smile as I walk into the room.

Mr. Dempsey's office is reminiscent of the Recency area. Dark, heavy mahogany wood furniture with extensive brass inlays and gilded metal accents. A large burgundy and cream Persian rug lays in the center of the room, worn from what looks like many years of use. The matching drapes exude a traditional feel of a long-ago estate. The scent of cigar smoke hangs in the air, although that may be more a figment of my imagination than actual smoke.

A deep, jovial voice interrupts my thoughts. "Ms. Kayleigh O'Reilly, so nice to meet ya."

I half expect him to be wearing a cravat and waistcoat, but the man sitting at the Carlton House desk has a green wool sweater, over a dress shirt, and plaid bow tie sticking out from the white collar. He's a stocky man with a bald head and wire-framed eyeglasses. His ruddy checks are full, and he has the same bright blue eyes as his daughter.

"Hello, Mr. Dempsey. It's a pleasure to meet you."

He rises from his padded chair and shakes my hand. "Please have a seat."

I sit on the floral chair, smoothing my gray pinstripe pencil skirt. I twist the pearl wrist button on my dusty blue button-down before folding my hands in my lap.

"So, let's get right to it." He leans back in his chair and lays his hands over his protruding stomach. "Why do ya want this job?"

"I want to find my inspiration again." It's not what I rehearsed, but I feel the truth in it.

Something between surprise and appreciation crosses his face. "Go on."

"My life changed the day before I left for Ireland. Everything I thought I knew and wanted in my life now feels wrong, and I'm not sure why. I feel different, and I'm not sure who I am anymore." I realize this is completely wrong for a job interview. I shouldn't be saying these things to a man I don't know. I'm not sure if it was meeting Fiadh, and her confidence that I belong here, or just opening myself up for the unexpected, but I want this job more than I thought.

I remind myself that this is still a job interview, and I need to provide my credentials. "I was a reporter for my high school newspaper the first two years and editor the second two. I'm in the *Saints and Scholars* program at Emerald Isle where Professor Gaffney is my mentor. I planned on writing for the university newspaper but...well, it wasn't a good fit."

He raises his eyebrows. "And ya think the Cloverdale Herald is a good fit for ya?"

"I don't know," I say honestly. "But I hope so." I reach into my bag for the portfolio and slide it across the desk. "I hope that after reading my sample writing and article proposal, you will feel the same way."

He leans forward and opens the portfolio. Pushing aside my writing samples, he removes the article proposal. Adjusting his glasses, he scans the page before replacing the paper and closing the portfolio. He sits back in his chair and looks out of the window.

Where I expect would have been nerves is a peace. A graceful peace. Maybe Fiadh was right and can see me better than I could see myself.

He clears his throat. "I'm goin' to give ya a chance, Kayleigh O'Reilly. Somethin' tells me you're not only the writer for this position but that ya're on to somethin' here.

I'm a man that goes with my instincts." He nods to the port-folio. "I'm interested in where your story goes."

My heart leaps at his words, whether it's for the job or the story I'm not sure. Either way, it feels like a new beginning. The chance I have been looking for to start over.

"Thank you, Mr. Dempsey. I won't let you down."

"I believe that. Fiadh will be in touch to work out the details." He extends his hand. "Welcome to the Cloverdale Herald."

LATER THAT MORNING, Seamus comes to the cottage to fix another leaking pipe under the kitchen sink. He grumbles as he collects his tools about the many updates the cottage needs, but I think it's a part of its charm. I fill him in on the interview with Mr. Dempsey while he works.

"I meet Fiadh, the editor's daughter, today at too. She seems a bit lost, but I think she's just looking for her path." Something I know too well. "As I was leaving, she asked if I wanted to have some tea before I left. I joined her in the small sitting room off the side of the lobby. It was nice to talk with her. Turns out she dreams of being a writer too."

Seamus puts the wrench down, giving me his full atten-tion. "Ya two must've had a lot to talk about then."

"We did. I feel for her because she has this dream, but it seems so far off that it's like she's giving up on it."

"What makes ya say that?"

"She dropped out of secondary school, and while her father gave her a job at the paper, it's all administrative work, no writing. He told her that she can't expect to be handed a profession—that she has to prove herself."

"I can see his point." Seamus worked hard for everything that he has. He had to prove himself over and over to become who he is today. *Rocky Shore Fishing* is not just a dream of his but the result of years of work and sacrifice.

"I understand it too. But on the other hand, I think if she had a second chance she could do just that."

Seamus grins at me. "Second chances are big in yer family."

"You know us so well," I say playfully before becoming serious again. "Talking with Fiadh gave me an idea."

Seamus sits in the dining chair next to me. "What kind of idea?"

"The inspiring kind. There are so many people like Fiadh. They never have that professor or friend who encourages them and helps them to see all that they have to offer. Fiadh has a writer's heart—I can see it. I want to help her and others find their voices in writing."

Seamus tucks a strand of hair behind my ear. "Ya'd be perfect for that. Ya see the best in people, when others over-look 'em. Ya inspire me every day, so I know ya'd do the same for others."

His full, unconditional confidence stokes the fire within me. This is the first time in my life that I feel called to do something. I remember how Teagan never wavered in making her dream a reality with *Second Chances*.

My shoulders fall. The difference is Teagan's talent was never in question. I can't say the same for mine. "It's just, I feel a little bit like a fraud. You read my recent writing. You saw Professor Gaffney's critiques. How can I help others discover their voice when I can't even find mine?"

"My Kayleigh," Seamus murmurs. "Ya're far more worthy than ya give yerself credit for. Ya have a writer's heart just the same."

His Kayleigh? My heart, a writer's or not, swells.

"That means so much."

He takes my hand in his. "Ya'll find yer voice again, and I hope I can help ya just like ya want to help Fiadh."

I think about the book nook and dreams I've had about creating the perfect place for writing. "I want to create a writing nook of sorts. A place where writers can go to get help with their writing and find peace to allow the words to come without distraction."

"A business?"

"I guess, but not in that business way. More like a community. I don't know anything about starting a business anyway, and I don't have any start-up money or anything." I slump in my chair.

"I may know a thing or two about business," he reminds me. "I'd be happy to help ya get started with plans."

Somehow I knew he would be here for me. "I was hoping you'd say that." I give his arm a playful push. "It's really just an idea for now.

"A good idea. One ya shouldn't let go." There's a longing in his eyes as he looks at me. "A dream is a special thing. It shouldn't be pushed aside. They're meant to be explored. How many of us dream every day without the hope of it ever comin' true?" His eyes drift to my lips.

I lean in closer to him. "And what dream do you want to come true?"

There's only a few inches between us. "I think my dream is about to come true."

His lips graze mine. So much is said in his soft touch, and I wonder how I ever could have thought love wasn't for me anymore. Just as I pull him closer, a loud knock sounds at the door.

Colonel runs to the window, nails scraping against the hardwood floor.

"Seamus, ya here?" A man's voice calls from outside.

"Eject." Seamus curses the man as he stands. Then he looks back at me. "I'm sorry."

My heart drops. "For kissing me?"

"What are ya jokin'? No! For Cormac interrupting us. He's here to help me fix the bloody pipe."

———

SEAMUS INTRODUCES me to the Kavanagh's new farm hand, Cormac. He's tall with broad shoulders and sandy blond hair and a matching stubble on his strong jawline. His light blue eyes have a mysterious quality to them, and his nose is slightly crooked, as if it was broken at one time.

When Seamus and Cormac put away their tools, the pipe no longer leaks. While they worked another idea forms. They join me at the table, each of them picking up a strawberry scone.

"I have an idea." I sit up straight in the chair, determined to convince Seamus that my idea is a good one.

"Ya're having lots of those recently." He takes a bite. "What's this new idea?"

"I think we should visit the shop. I need to be there to get the right feeling for the article."

"What shop?"

"*O'Doherty and Brannan's Pot o' Gold*, of course."

He looks like this is the last thing he wants to do right now.

"Come on," I coax, "you're always saying how you need to take advantage of the good weather in Ireland, and all that. Well, look outside it's beautiful."

"I really need to watch what I say more." He finishes his scone.

"So, will you take me?"

He rustles the hair on Colonel's head, who tries to lick the remaining crumbs off of his hand. "It's about a three-hour drive."

"I could use the time to study, and Colonel loves car rides," I plead before turning to Cormac for reinforcement. "What do you think?"

He shrugs. "I'd be up for a drive."

Seamus shoots him a look that has me covering my mouth to hold back the laugh. "I have a feelin' I'm goin' to regret this."

"Yes!" I jump up and throw my arms around him.

Looks like my research is about to get real.

CHAPTER EIGHT

When we arrive in County Donegal, the sun continues to shine, but there are dark clouds lurking in the distance. The shop that used to be *O'Doherty and Brannan's Pot o' Gold* is located in the small northern town of Elderstone. The road and walkways are ancient cobblestone, giving a feel of antiquity. The walkways lead to homes and family-owned shops made of a combination of Scots pine and local stone.

"Well, the name seems appropriate," I remark as we pass an old stone bakery.

Seamus turns onto a narrow street and nods towards the houses we pass. "The Irish have always been a proud people. Our heritage is somethin' that is passed down through the generations. Here in Elderstone, a large granite stone is considered the metaphorical rock of the community. It's good luck to touch it as ya pass by."

"A superstition, huh?"

"Superstition and faith can sometimes be blurred in these areas."

"Which do you believe it is?"

He waves a hand in the air. "I'm an Irishman, Kayleigh,

my faith is as strong as Aunt Nora's tea. But, I won't be walkin' under any ladders if that's what ya're gettin' at."

I laugh. "Okay, I see how it is."

"I'd like to see the Elderstone," Cormac says from the back seat.

"Is it a big tourist attraction?" I ask, my curiosity peaking.

"Don't think so," he replies, "but granite is one of my favorite stones to work with."

I think back to the glass jar he made that holds my lavender water. "Why is granite so special?"

His eyes light up at the topic. "Granite's an igneous rock which crystallizes as it cools, breaking down to its mineral components."

"What minerals?"

"A glassy quartz, a white or pink feldspar, and a black or silvery mica. The combination of the three is outstanding."

Seamus' lips quirk, and I know that no matter how annoyed he acted towards Cormac earlier, he enjoys his company. And I feel the same. Cormac is a true artist, seeing what others can miss in the commonality of it all. To me it's just stone, but to Cormac it's art.

"This area is known for its rocks," Seamus adds. "I haven't the faintest clue about 'em, but Cormac does."

"Aye," Cormac agrees with more enthusiasm than I've seen him have yet. "There's Precambrian metamorphic rocks, the granites, lower carboniferous sandstones, and of course the limestone."

"Do you do a lot of masonry in addition to blowing glass?"

Colonel stretches out on the backseat, his back legs settling on Cormac's lap. "I do my fair share, but glass blowing is hard to beat."

"I'm sure it is. It sounds fascinating. My sister Ashling is always talking about wanting to learn to stain glass.

"'Tis a fine skill."

"You'll have to show Ashling one day. She doesn't get excited for many things, but that would be something even she couldn't hold back on."

Cormac looks out of the window. "I'm not much of a teacher."

"Everyone's a good teacher when they love the subject," I tell him.

We pull up alongside a stone gate at the end of an alleyway. A shop is straight ahead and to the right with its boarded-up windows and a faded sign hanging above the door that reads *O'Doherty and Brannan's Pot o' Gold*.

"I wonder why their family never sold the shop."

"No idea." Seamus shakes his head. "It's been closed for almost twenty years now. The neighbors can't be too happy to have it lookin' like this."

"It was in their will."

We look at Cormac. When he doesn't say any more I ask, "What was in the will?"

"That the shop wouldn't be sold until the right person came along. They couldn't bear the thought of the shop being anythin' other than a place of art. Heard about it a long time ago and never forgot 'cause it's a bit crazy."

"That it is," Seamus says.

"Wait," I say, trying to understand, "who determines who the right person is and how can they even judge that?"

"No idea." Cormac shrugs as if the thought never occurred to him.

Seamus cuts the engine. "Well, let's go check it out."

"Seamus, you see it. It's all boarded up." I point to the building.

When I look back at them they're both grinning, and I get the feeling that whatever we're about to do will be an adventure.

We walk around to the back of the building. The contrast between this shop and the surrounding shops is great. Where the other shops gleam with cleanliness and activity, *O'Doherty and Brannan's Pot o' Gold* looks as deserted as a shop abandoned twenty years ago would look. The back alleyway is clear of debris, but graffiti marks the door and window boards.

"The stone is untouched." I run my fingers over the area right beside the door. It's as if the one painting the graffiti couldn't break the unspoken bond to the stone.

Neither Seamus nor Cormac comment on this, but rather they continue using a pin to pick the padlock. Colonel sits by me, scanning the area. The street is empty as the shops are all closed. Once the shops close, there's no reason for anyone to be here.

There's a clicking sound followed by a pop. Seamus jiggles the lock, pulling the two metal claps apart. "We're good. Let's get inside before someone sees somethin'."

"I haven't seen any sign of anyone. And Colonel hasn't made a sound." It's like my words are wishing it to be the truth.

"There's always someone around." Cormac's remark does little to ease my nerves.

The door hinge screeches as Seamus pries it open, and we slide inside. We turn on our flashlights and take in the main room. Glass display cases line the two side walls and front bay window. I walk towards the window and can imagine the selection of jewelry that once awaited its owner. Everything I have learned about Michael and James points to a unique business with one of a kind artisan items. When you purchased a piece of jewelry here, there was meaning behind it. No two pieces would've been the same.

I shine the flashlight around the room. "Even with the cobwebs and dust, there's something special about this place."

"Ya're right about that." Seamus examines a floor lamp in the corner. Its gold base and bubble glass shade shine even after all of these years.

"I think this is where they made the jewelry." Cormac is still standing in the little cove we entered from the back. While it leads directly into the main room, there's a section partition. "The tools and remnants of metal are in these drawers."

"Do you think there used to be a wall here?" I wave my hand along the three-foot-high divider.

"It may have been, but I think they worked in the open." Cormac puts a few pieces of metal into the drawer.

"You think people watched them?" I try to imagine the scene.

He scans the area again. "I do. It would've made the shop a part of the community. Customers could see the items as they were crafted."

I think back to the day I watched Ashling painting a landscape of the orchard last summer. I watched as she mixed the watercolors for the perfect shade, using water to blend the colors to create her own version of the scene. "It would've been part of what made the jewelry and the shop unique."

"I believe so." Cormac rubs a piece of metal wire between his fingers. "It must have been a sight back in the day."

"Yeah. It's a shame it ended up this way."

"I wonder if there are any remaining personal items or paperwork left." I look around the dusty room.

"I think an office may be at the top of these stairs." Seamus stands at the bottom of the flight of stairs looking up. Colonel seems to understand the importance and pushes his way past Seamus and takes two steps at a time.

We follow Colonel into a large upper room. Two twin bed

frames sit on either side of the far side, a window in the middle. The mattresses are missing, but the frames show wear.

"They lived here." I walk closer to the empty bed frames.

"Probably easier to work on the pieces," Cormac says.

"And they would've been saving more than a few bobs staying here. One payment for the business and apartment," Seamus agrees.

"Jacks over here." Cormac points to the dated bathroom with a small standing shower. The shower curtain is missin', but a few metal rings hang from the rod. The sink and toilet are yellowed and give off a slight scent of mildew.

Framed photos line the wall, each skewed in various degrees. I brush the dust off of one photo revealing the smiling faces of two young men. One has curly dark hair and matching eyes while the other has rich brown hair and light green eyes. They both have black rain slickers zipped up to their chins. They are standing in front of the shop pointing to the new sign.

"It's from the day they opened the shop," I murmur to myself.

Seamus walks up beside me. "Look like it." He points to the man with brown hair. "That must be Michael. He resembles Caitlin."

I look closer. "He does." Which means the dark-haired man is James Brannan. "It's odd seeing them together like this."

"That's what we need." Cormac gestures to the traveling street vendor with a *Fish & Chips* sign. "I'll be back with sustenance."

"How can you think of your stomach at a time like this?" Seamus waves a hand in the air.

"It's easy. I'm hungry and that's food. I'll bring us some

back." Cormac descends the stairs, and the screen door snaps shut.

"Eejit better not get caught." He walks back to the desk along the back wall.

I take out my phone and snap a photo of the two men before following Seamus.

"Looks like a lot of paperwork." He shifts through the drawer.

I don't respond because I'm looking at a gold framed photo sitting on the desk. Michael has his arm around a slight woman with shoulder-length light red curls and hazel eyes. Her fair skin is sprinkled with freckles, and her natural peach-colored lips are stretched in a wide grin as he kisses her. Her left hand holds his cheek, and a bright sapphire stone sits in a granite inlay on the gold band. Is it an engagement ring?

"Their finances were strong. There's no evidence that they had any financial issues." Seamus closes a logbook.

"Seamus, look at this." I pass him the framed photo.

"Looks like we may have found our woman." He takes the back off of the frame.

"What are you doing?"

He holds up the back of the photo. "Lookin' for this."

Michael and Maeve
Forever

Below the handwritten words is a heart. In the center, two sets of initials.

M.O.

+

M.S.

"I think they were engaged."

"I think yer right," Seamus agrees. "The question is, did they go through with it?"

A loud rumbling sounds in front of the store. Seamus peers out of the side of the window, standing carefully out of sight. "Motorbikes."

A flash of fear seeps through me. "Lots of people have motorbikes," I say, trying to reassure myself as much as Seamus. "It doesn't mean it's Nathair."

"Looks like Nathair," Seamus grumbles.

So much for reassurance. "What do we do?"

"Nothin' to do. Just wait 'em out." His eyes narrow. "Wait a minute. What is he doin'?"

I move to Seamus' side and peer through the window.

Cormac crosses the road carrying three trays of fish and chips. As he reaches the other side, two men dressed all in black walk over to him. He stops and turns toward them.

"Why's he talking to them?"

A muscle flexes in Seamus' jaw. "Don't know."

"Does he know them?"

Seamus doesn't respond.

"If he would just turn a little towards us, we could see his expression."

The heavier of the two men hands Cormac a small brown paper bag. After a moment, Cormac tucks the bag into the pocket of his brown leather jacket and continues walking towards the jewelry store.

"Should we ask him about it?"

A muscle twitches in Seamus' jaw. "I'm not sure how much Uncle Malachy and Aunt Nora have told him."

The back door screeches open and shut.

Seamus' hands are balled into fists.

"Just because Ryan betrayed you doesn't mean Cormac will do the same," I warn, before either of us jump to conclusions.

Seamus steps away from the window. "I think it's time to go home."

I slip the framed photograph into my bag. We meet Cormac downstairs and take the food with us for the ride home. The drive home is quiet, and I watch Colonel carefully to see how he reacts to Cormac. He's the best judge of character that I know. If Cormac can't be trusted, wouldn't Colonel sense it, or is fried fish too big of a temptation for the dog? He happily accepts a piece of fish from Cormac, wagging his tail, seemingly without a worry in the world.

Cormac catches me watching them and I quickly look away, no longer sure who we can trust.

***

THE NEXT EVENING, I sit at the kitchen table rereading my article for the third time.

"Read it and let me know what you think." I pass the laptop to Seamus.

The memory of the last time he read my writing is fresh in my mind. I pray this time there's a better reception. As he reads the article, his expression remains neutral. When he finally looks up, there's excitement in his eyes. "It's grand."

"Really?"

"Really. Ya pulled me in from the first lines. The story is interesting, but it's the writing...this has heart."

"So, do you think Mr. Dempsey will publish it?

"He can't pass it up." He slides the laptop back to me.

I click the send button. "Now what?"

Seamus takes my hand in his. "Now, we wait."

We settle into our own rhythm cleaning up the kitchen. A half hour later, the familiar ding of a new message sounds.

I flip open my laptop, and the unread message stares back at me. "That was quick. He's replied."

"What are ya waitin' for? Open it."

The cursor hangs over the new message, but I can't bring myself to click it. What if it's more rejection? What if he tells me I can't write and that I have no business trying?

"Kayleigh?" Seamus puts the last dish away and looks at me expectantly.

"You do it. I can't." I turn away from the message.

Seamus leans over the laptop. "Alright."

He clicks on the message. After what feels like an eternity, but is probably only a minute or two, I throw up my hands. "Well? What does it say?"

"Turn around." His tone isn't even giving away anything.

When I do, he grins at me. "He loves the idea. A teaser of the story is goin' to be published in this Saturday's paper."

I throw my arms around Seamus' neck, and he wraps his strong arms around me, pulling me in close.

"Looks like you're a full-fledged reporter." His breath tickles my neck.

"Yup." I lay my head against his chest. The steady beating of his heart reminds me that while this is great news, I'm still not sure if journalism is even right for me.

"I should get going." He kisses the top of my head and grabs his cargo jacket. "Early mornin' on the sea tomorrow."

I miss his warmth immediately. "Okay. I'll see you soon?"

"Very soon." He gives Colonel a pat on the head before closing the cottage door behind him.

I'm left standing there, wishing his arms were still around me again.

I JOIN Colonel on the rug by the fire later that night. I set the laptop on the floor next to me, hoping for some kind of inspiration for my story for Professor Gaffney's class. Maybe I'm just not cut out to be a novelist. That's not such a bad thing, I guess. I do have the job at the newspaper now, and I would still be writing.

Just not the stories I want to write.

Colonel lays his big head on my lap, and I stroke his wiry fur. I watch the flames dancing in the fireplace. Each flame moves on its own, but together they create something brilliant. And then an idea sparks like an ember from the fire. I know what story I need to write for the *Saints and Scholars* program. More precisely, I know *whose* story I need to write. In all of my writing, I have always focused on other people's stories. It's time I focus on my story.

I open the laptop. Tonight, I begin to write my own story.

"I CAN'T BELIEVE you wrote this without telling us!" Teagan paces back and forth across the small sitting room. "I mean, it's one thing to find out these details and talk to us about it, but to actually publish it in the paper...and knowing that Nathair's watching everything..." She stares off into space.

It's Saturday evening and we're at the Kavanaghs. The story teaser for my article was published this morning, and the response isn't what I hoped it would be.

"It's a small-town paper, maybe the repercussions will be small," Finn says optimistically.

Teagan throws her hands up. "Small? The way words spread around here, all of Ireland probably knows."

"I'm sorry." My voice is weak. What did I think would happen? I was so focused on getting the job and being the first to share the story that I disregarded the people most important to me. An image of Jamie from that day in Magnolia's cafe flashes through my mind. She just wanted the story too.

"It's my fault. I should've considered this." Seamus sits on the sofa beside me. "I didn't think how it would look to Nathair. We know the shop holds a clue to who's behind all of this, but I should've known better."

Finn puts a hand on Teagan's arm before she can say anything more. "We know it wasn't intentional. I just wonder why you guys went to the shop in the first place."

I glance at Cormac standing by the doorway. He has a mug in his hand and doesn't appear to be as unnerved as the rest of us.

I shrug. "The story is fascinating, and I wanted to learn what caused Michael and James to dissolve their friendship and close the shop."

"I know." Teagan sighs. "It's just now, it looks like we're provoking Nathair, and it's not time to do that yet."

Yet? Dread turns my stomach.

"I think we need to look ahead and figure out what we should do now," Finn says.

"Right ya are," Nora agrees. "Don't be mindin' what's done." She smiles at me. "And ya're not wrong, dear. Somethin' does need to be done. The question that remains is what we should be doin'."

"I'll call Garda Connell," Malachy says firmly. "He'll know best what our next step should be."

Teagan sits on the arm of the sofa and wraps her arm

around me. Her warmth almost triggers the tears welling in my eyes. How could I have been so blind in my reporting?

"Do you trust this newspaper?" Teagan asks, breaking into my thoughts.

I picture Mr. Dempsey and Fiadh—their sincere and honest dispositions. "Yes. I really do. They didn't know the implications of this. I obviously didn't think it through either. Mr. Dempsey is a good guy, and his family is one who can be trusted."

Teagan's lips twist to the side in that way that tells me she's thinking deeply about something.

"What is it?" I ask.

She shrugs. "If they are as good as you say, maybe they can help us in the future."

And with those words, I wonder what the future may hold.

A FEW WEEKS LATER, I look into the oval mirror of the vanity in the corner of the bedroom. It's Christmas Eve, and things have been quiet. It's a relief but suspicious at the same time. I dust my cheeks with pink blush and apply matching lip gloss. My hair falls in big curly waves over my shoulder, and I darken my navy eyeliner for a moody look. After clipping on my gold heart earrings, I dab a few drops of the lavender water on my wrists and neck.

When I take Colonel outside for a quick walk, he does his normal survey of the yard before he stops and stares off in the distance. I follow his gaze to the bay and spot a man standing on the dock. He's dressed in a black fishing coat and khaki pants, with a black wool beanie on his head. And he's staring right at me.

The man holds a hand up and I freeze.

He's back.

A high-pitched ringing fills my ears, and Colonel's bark sounds faraway. I shake my head to clear the brain fog and then pull Colonel into the cottage, my heart pounding in my chest. I lean against the door trying to catch my breath. After a few moments Colonel jumps up at the window and puts his front paws on the ledge. His tail flies from side to side as he whines in excitement.

It's not the reaction I expected given the mysterious man on the dock.

"Kayleigh!"

The deep voice sounds familiar. "Seamus?"

"Kayleigh, what're ya doin'?"

I pull the door open, and Seamus stands with his hands in his pockets and confusion in his eyes below the black wool beanie.

"Ya look like you've seen a ghost." He reaches for me.

"I..." I step aside and let him into the cottage. "I thought you were someone else."

The lines deepen around his eyes. "Who'd ya think I was?"

How do I tell him without causing more alarm. "A little while back," I say tentatively, "I saw a man, dressed all in black, standing on the dock."

His body tenses. "When?"

"I don't remember exactly. A while ago. But, he just stared at me before getting on his jet ski and speeding away. Do you think it could have been Nathair?"

"Lots of folks have jet skis 'round here." He loosens the scarf around his neck.

"I'll be fine," I assure him. When he doesn't look convinced, I nod to Colonel. "I do have him, after all."

He eyes Colonel, and the tension in his shoulders eases ever so slightly.

"Why were you on the dock?" I ask, trying to lighten the mood. The last thing I want to do is carry this apprehension into the evening.

"I thought ya may want to go by boat to theceilidh."

"Oh." I pause, considering the somewhat mild sixty-degree weather for December. The sky is clear, and it would be nice to be on the water, as long as it's not too cold.

"Don't ya worry, the cabin is heated. Ya won't catch a chill."

I laugh at his intuitiveness. "Then I'm in."

He pulls me into a warm embrace, the scent of saltwater and peppermint calming my nerves. The cold is an afterthought in his warmth. The evening may have gotten off to a rough start, but I have a feeling tonight will be one to remember.

CHAPTER NINE

As we walk through the castle doors, warm candle lighting and rustic tables welcome us. Twinkling fairy lights sparkle from the wood beams and boughs of fresh evergreen and ivy are strewn about the walls. The scent of pine recalls memories of past Christmases. Christmas has always been my favorite holiday. There's something so special about a dark and quiet Christmas Eve. The image of Mary cuddling baby Jesus, surrounded by the lowing of the cattle. Joseph standing strong by her side. No love story could ever compare. Looking around the hall tonight, it feels like more than a celebration—the room is decorated as a tribute to that first Christmas Eve. A manger is set up in the front of the hall. A warm spotlight shines on the scene.

A man croons into a microphone as a band plays traditional Irish folk carols from the corner. Townspeople sit on wooden chairs at the long wooden tables. A long centerpiece of white candles and ivy with red berries adorn the tables, bringing a glow to the smiling faces—including two faces I haven't seen in over four months.

"Mom! Dad!" I hurry to their table, and I am immediately taken into a giant hug from Dad and given a kiss from Mom.

"Kayleigh, you are glowing!" Mom twirls me around.

"Thanks. It's probably the candles." I tuck a strand of hair behind my ear.

She shakes her head. "No. A candle can't give off that kind of glow." She holds my face between her hands, running her thumb over my cheek.

Her eyes stop on someone behind me, and her smile grows even wider. "Seamus, so good to see you again!" This time it's her chance for a big hug while Dad shakes his hand.

"Always a pleasure," Seamus replies, his Irish lilt sounding stronger than normal. "How long will ye be stayin'?" He looks genuinely happy to see them, and I would be lying if that doesn't do things with my heart.

"A week," Dad replies, bobbing his head to the music. "We'll leave in time to get Ashling back for school."

"School and we need to check on the farm. A week away is a long time, even with the best caretakers in the world." Mom wraps her arm through Dad's.

"Uncle Malachy will never leave Brigid's Crossing for even a day without worrying. Aunt Nora, on the other hand, talks about visitin' the Caribbean one of these winters."

"Ah, the warm weather would be wonderful this time of year," Mom agrees. "But, I feel for Malachy. It's hard to let go of something that means so much to you, even for a short time."

"Aye, I can understand that." Seamus' eyes flash to me. "Although, the sun may be a wee bit too strong for our Irish skin."

"There you are." Ashling joins us with a fizzy apple drink. She is dressed in fitted black pants and a flowy green tunic top. Her long silky auburn hair is pulled back on the sides with two braids that reveal golden strawberry-hued highlights. Her green eyes dance with excitement, but her demeanor is as laid-back as ever.

"Ashling!" I wrap my arms around her, nearly spilling her drink.

"Oh, great. The hugging has begun." Her tone is flat, but I hear the faint smile in her voice.

I give her a playful push. Ashling acts like she doesn't care, but I know she does, just in her own way.

"Hi Seamus. Nice to see you again." She gives him a playful nudge with her elbow. "I hope you've been keeping Kayleigh company."

"Alright, let's get some food before the dancing begins," I say, taking Seamus' hand and pulling him along with me to the buffet table. I don't miss the look of approval on Ashling's face.

We fill our plates with Dublin Bay prawns, diced potatoes, gravy, carrots, and brussels sprouts before sitting at the table. Just as we begin eating, Teagan and Finn walk in with Cormac.

"Sorry we're late," Teagan says as she removes her heavy down jacket and slides in next to Ashling. "This is Cormac Byrne. He's the new farrier at the farm."

"So nice to meet you, Cormac," Mom says as she cuts into the gamey meat. "I know we just missed you when we arrived at the farm. I'm Molly O'Reilly, and this is my husband, Patrick."

Dad gives a wave as he takes another scoop of potatoes.

"My parents are visiting for the week," Teagan tells him. "And this is our youngest sister, Ashling."

Cormac gives Ashling a brief glance. "Pleasure." After a moment of awkward silence, he excuses himself to the buffet table.

"So, he shoes the horses?" Dad asks.

Seamus takes a gulp of his ale. "That and all kinds of metal work. He's got a gift for glass blowin' too."

"Yes!" My reaction has everyone turning to me. "Teagan and I picked up these fragrances at one of the Cloverdale markets. Lavender for me and orange blossom for Teag, and the seller was his sister. She told us how he made all of the glass jars for the scents."

"The bottles are incredibly intricate," Teagan agrees. "He goes down to Mr. Brennan's glass shop in town to work in the studio."

Ashling glances towards the buffet, eyes settling on Cormac. "Glass blowing is an awesome art. I've always wanted to see it in person."

"Not another one." Dad jokes, before Mom shooshes him.

Ashling appears to not have heard him or is ignoring the comment. "Too bad we won't be here long enough to check it out."

"There's always next year," I remind her.

"Next year?" Seamus asks.

"Ashling will be joining Emerald Isle in their Fine Arts program in the fall. She won an art scholarship for early admission."

"Is that right? Congratulations to ya, Ashling."

"Thanks." She shifts in her seat.

"That's a lot of O'Reilly sisters at Emerald Isle. Think the university will still be standin'?"

"Oh, you love the O'Reilly sisters," Teagan says.

"Don't mean to be interruptin'," Nora says, sliding in next to Teagan on the bench, "but I overheard ye talkin' about next year." She takes a moment to catch her breath, her cheeks pink with tiny beads of sweat. "I'm not as young as I once was, and these dance steps have me feelin' my age."

Nora wipes her forehead with a handkerchief. "Malachy and I would love to have Ashling stay with us in Teagan's old room, if she wishes, that is. It's not bein' used, and it's not too far a drive into Dublin."

"I'd love that!" Ashling says, without an ounce of hesitation. "Do you mean it?"

Nora's face beams. "Of course, dear. We'd love to have ya." She looks to Mom and Dad. "That is if it's alright with yer folks."

Mom takes her hand. "Nora, our family owes you and Malachy so much for the way you've taken care of our girls. We would be honored for her to stay with you. You all are our second family."

Nora's eyes shine. "We feel the same," she says, apparently straining to keep her emotions at bay.

Excitement radiates off Ashling, and while it is an exciting offer, Ashling jumped on the offer a little too quickly. A quick glance at Teagan tells me she's having similar thoughts.

Cormac chooses that moment to sit in the seat opposite Ashling. He sets his full plate on the table and slides his chair in without looking up.

"Ah, Cormac," Malachy calls over to him after having joined Nora on the opposite side of the table, "we'll be havin' Ashling joinin' us on the farm late summer. She'll be in the university's Fine Arts program next fall. Ya two have a lot in common."

"I never went to university." Cormac barely looks up but then seems to realize how abrupt he sounds. "What kind of art do ya do?"

Ashling takes a scoop of chocolate mousse. "Mostly watercolors, but I work some with ceramics too."

"Do you paint landscapes?" He asks with apprehension edging his voice.

"Sometimes, but usually people. I like capturing people's realness.

He stops eating and looks at her. "How do ya know what's real?"

"Let's dance!" Mom says, breaking the building tension. She pulls Dad onto the floor with Teagan and Finn in tow. People are forming groups of four for the next set.

"I bet Teagan has every dance perfected to the last step," Ashling says while watching them walk onto the dance floor.

Seamus and I laugh, remembering the last time we were at a ceilidh.

"Ya might be a little surprised," I tell her.

Now intrigued, Ashling turns her chair around to face the dancers. "I am ready for a show."

"And I think she's about to get one," Seamus whispers. "Maybe we should show 'em how it's done."

"The next one," I promise.

Teagan and Finn circle around, stepping on each other's toes and bumping into other couples.

"It's a fine thing their research doesn't involve 'em dancing," Malachy quips.

"Seeing her like this does my heart good." Nora holds a hand over her heart.

"Me too." I watch as Teagan laughs while Finn swings her around and around. "It's time she let loose and have some fun."

These are the moments that matter. Moments when you know you'll look back and wish you could live them again. Seeing Teagan so carefree and happy is wonderful. It's all about little moments like these with the people who mean the most to you. I've never felt like I belong more than I do in this moment in a centuries-old Irish castle.

After the song ends, the guys go to get another round of pints while Mom and Ashling join the next jig, leaving me and Nora alone.

"Is everything alright?" She gives me her full attention.

"Yes." I blink back tears. "I'm just really happy having everyone together."

She nods in understanding. "Nothin' better than family."

"I keep thinking that someone's going to get hurt. Do you think Nathair is capable of real harm?"

She reaches for my hand. "Now, now, dear. Don't ya be worrin' about 'em on this holy night. We can get through anythin' as long as we have faith. We always have, and we always will."

Faith.

"The thing is...I'm not sure I have any faith left in me."

Nora chuckles. "Ya're a woman of faith. I knew it the moment I saw ya. 'She has a heart of gold' I told Malachy that day. It's the God's honest truth."

"How would you know that? Sometimes I feel like I don't have the same kind of faith as you."

"Ah, well, ya don't get to be my age without a whole lot of life experience. And one thin' this life has taught me is to know a good person when I see 'em. And ya are one of the good ones."

"To be honest, Nora, I don't know how strong my faith is at the moment."

She gives my hand a little squeeze. "We all go through that a time or two. The important thing is to never allow it to make you bitter and forget all of the good in this world."

Did I become bitter after my breakup with Chris? Yes. I wish the answer didn't come so quickly, but it's true. I allowed myself to become bitter because things weren't as I planned. All I saw was the betrayal and destruction of my dreams when I should have focused on God's plan instead. My sisters and my best friend all thought the breakup was a good thing. That should have told me right then and there that I was blind to so many things.

I spot Seamus across the room dancing with Mrs.

Murphy. The elderly lady shuffles her feet to the rhythm, turning with Seamus a few beats slower than the rest of the group. Seamus never falters in his steps though. He leads her with confidence and compassion. Her wrinkled face is lively as she laughs with Seamus. This dance is one of her moments.

Seamus is so different than Chris, but it doesn't make opening myself up again any easier.

"Try to trust Seamus, dear." Nora follows my gaze. "I see ya two together. There's somethin' there—somethin' you don't find every day."

"We're just friends," I say quickly, and realize how fake it sounds even to my own ears.

Nora leans back in her chair. "The greatest love starts as friendship."

"You sound like Magnolia. But, I don't think I'm ready for love again."

"Aye, it can be difficult after ya've been hurt so...but, it would be a shame to miss somethin' so beautiful."

"I think my relationship with Chris was more in my head than anything else. I had this ideal vision of what love should be, and I'm embarrassed to say it didn't really matter who the guy was. I missed a lot of signs that we weren't meant to be together, but if we broke up, it was like my dream would die." I shake my head. "I was such a fool—about so many things."

"We all are at one time or another." She looks like she's revisiting an old memory. "Just remember, when one dream dies, it gives room for another to come to life."

AT MIDNIGHT, the music stops, and the crowd gathers around the manger scene. Fr. Nolan leads the St. Andrew prayer, and the townspeople recite it with him twelve times.

"Hail and blessed be the hour and moment in which the

Son of God was born of the most pure Virgin Mary, at midnight, in Bethlehem, in the piercing cold. In that hour, vouchsafe, I beseech Thee, O my God, to hear my prayer and grant my desire, through the merits of Our Savior Jesus Christ, and of His Blessed Mother. Amen."

Our voices fill the hall as the music did just moments ago. I've never felt more a part of something in all my life.

"And now, as tradition for hundreds of years, it's time to wish baby Jesus a very happy birthday."

A cheer goes up as a round of *Happy Birthday* echoes throughout the grand room. When the singing fades, people place tiny wrapped objects and cards at the foot of the manger.

"What are they doing?" Ashling asks.

"They are giving symbolic gifts to baby Jesus." Teagan says, pulling out a birthday card from her bag. "Let's write our gifts together."

She starts by scribbling in the card. "I give you *Second Chances* and all of our passion and work. I hope we help people through You."

She hands Ashling the card next. "I give You my art and creativity. I hope my creations echo the beauty of Yours."

"I love that," Teagan says with an encouraging smile. "That's the perfect gift, Ash."

I take the card and pen but don't write anything. As they watch me expectantly, I swallow the lump in my throat.

"You two are giving your dreams to Jesus, but the thing is —I don't know what my dream is anymore. How can I give something that I don't know that I even have?"

"So, give what you *do* have," Teagan says, as practical as ever. "A gift from the heart is always the best kind."

My heart may have been broken, but slowly the pieces are coming back together. "I give you my heart. Take these broken pieces and mend them to love again. Plant in my heart the seed of love so a new dream can grow."

"That's beautiful, Kay." Teagan wraps her arm around my shoulder and gives it a squeeze.

"Well, of course hers is all poetic. She is the writer, after all." Ashling rolls her eyes, and we laugh.

We place the birthday card with our gifts at the foot of the manager before returning to our table. As we gather our things, a phone rings. Malachy reaches into the pocket of his worn green tweed jacket.

"I'll never get used to these things." He pulls out a silver cell phone and slides on his reading glasses. "It's Mac." His eyebrows furrow as he answers the call.

Seamus stops cleaning the table and watches Malachy.

"Who's Mac?" I whisper to him.

"Uncle Malachy's mate from school. He works at the town bank and oversees the farm," Seamus tells me.

Silence descends upon the table.

"Get off with ya! Couldn't be." Malachy rubs a hand over his head as if trying to clear it. "No, no. Ya did the right thing. Thanks for callin', Mac. Keep me updated, 'right."

More silence.

"Aye, ya too. Send our best to the family and Merry Christmas."

He ends the call and slides the phone back into his pocket with a tremble in his hands. He leans back in his chair without uttering a word.

"Get on with ya!" Nora urges, pulling her shawl close around her. "What did Mac say? Come out with it already."

"The bank..." He runs a hand through his thick white hair. "Collapsed."

Nora gasps. "Collapsed? How's that so?"

His eyes look down before meeting hers, sadness evident in their depths. "Mr. Colin Banwell has takin' control."

CHAPTER TEN

The week following Christmas is subdued with the news of the bank collapse. I run through the motions of sightseeing with my family, but there's a tension in the air.

"So, your parents and Ashling are home safe now?" Magnolia asks over the phone at the end of the week.

"Yeah. They got in earlier this morning."

The sound of soft country music plays in the background, and I can picture Magnolia cleaning up from the breakfast rush.

"How are things at home?"

"Okay. You know it's always busy during the holidays, so I hired on extra help. I am leaving operations in their capable hands so I can go upstairs now so we can talk in peace."

I picture her quaint loft, and part of me wishes I could be there with her. We would curl up on her oversized couch, drinking tea and catching up for hours.

The door of the loft closes, and she exhales deeply. "Nothing new here in Berryville. Although, I did hear there is a new vet in town. I haven't met him yet though."

"My parents' veterinary intern. They mentioned he would be starting in the new year."

"Nancy Miller was around this morning. She said she was coming by to pick up a warm apple tart, but I think it was more to gossip. She didn't take a bite of the tart, and when she left, it was still sitting on the counter."

I laugh. Nancy Miller is the middle-aged widow of the late mayor, and she's president of the town's garden society. She also holds the well-earned title of official town gossip. If there's something, or someone, new in town, you can bet Ms. Miller will be the first to share the news. She considers it her duty to the community.

"So, what was she gossiping about today?"

"Not what but who—the new vet, of course."

"Of course. Well, what does she know so far?" I wonder how much is truth and how much is her speculation.

"Surprisingly little. Just that he's from Boston and staying at Roy Johnson's old cabin by the lake. Apparently, he's fixing the place up."

"It's good someone's in that cabin. It used to be so nice, but when his wife passed away, and then he went into the assisted living, the cabin was left abandoned."

"It is at the prettiest place by the lake. By the sound of it, he likes his peace and privacy."

"Can't blame him for that. My parents said that after Boston College, he attended their alma mater, Roisin University in Ithaca, New York. I think that's how he found them, since they're in the alumni directory. They said as soon as they met him, they knew he would fit right in on the farm."

"He sounds intriguing. I'm looking forward to meeting this Dr. Carson soon. I mean, he can't hide in our small town too long."

"That's true. He'll be a part of the community whether he likes it or not."

We laugh knowing it's completely true. As much as the cottage and Ireland feel like home to me, I know a part of me will always be in Berryville. I can't imagine being away from my hometown for too long, but for now, I call Colonel, and we go for a long walk down by the bay.

***

A COUPLE OF WEEKS LATER, we are all at Brigid's Crossing for the Kavanagh's Sunday dinner. Nora made one of her favorite family recipes of boiled bacon, cabbage, and potatoes. A hearty white sauce tops the meals and gives the simple dish a unique flavor.

"We still don't know how Banwell fits into all of this." Finn takes a bite of bacon before continuing. "Seems he no longer spends his time at the university, but we can't tell if he is still on the board anymore or not."

"It's all very odd." Teagan scoops more sauce onto her potatoes. "Zoey and Kyle almost didn't make their departure to the Galápagos Islands because their forms were left unsigned. At the last minute another board member signed the necessary documentation, but it was close."

"I'm glad they were still able to go." I remember how excited Zoey and Kyle were for the chance to continue their research on the islands for the semester. "I'm sure you guys will miss having your roommates though."

I, on the other hand, would not know that feeling. I will always be grateful to Seamus for offering me the cottage, and a chance out of my dorm room. How different this school year would have been if I was stuck in that situation. I wonder if I would still be in Ireland at all.

"It's different without Zoey for sure, but I know this chance is something they couldn't pass up. To apply their research in one of the most incredible places in the world is just unreal. They have a real chance of having their research published."

"That's amazing," I say, not sure that I fully grasp the scientific meaning of it all, but I do know how wonderful it would be to have my writing published.

"Traveling to the Galápagos is a great opportunity for both of them," Finn says. "And Kyle was packing like he was not only going on a research trip but a vacation too."

"Same with Zoey," Teagan agrees. "You should have seen her deciding on clothes. I think with some of her outfits she was more worried about style than of biting bugs and the weather. While her sundresses are adorable, they won't help her much with the bugs or sun. I think this trip is a little more than just a research project for her too."

I laugh along with everyone else at the thought of Zoey and Kyle together all semester in such a beautiful place. "It does sound very romantic."

"I guess romantic," Teagan says, "but definitely itchy."

Finn puts his fork down and looks at Teagan. "Romantic *you guess?* That's all? You wouldn't find a semester in one of the most beautiful islands in the world romantic?"

"Okay," she says with a laugh. "Yes, it could be romantic."

"Romantic enough to throw caution to the wind and skip the bug protection and pack a sundress or two?" Finn asks.

Now everyone is looking at Teagan. "Well, that's just foolishness. You can be romantic and still practical." When we all laugh, she continues. "Maybe we should visit them during spring break and test our theories."

Finn's raises an eyebrow. "Are you serious?"

"Sure, why not?" She takes a bite of bacon before shooting him a challenging look.

His gaze holds hers. "We'll book the tickets today."

"I'll start packing the sundresses—*and* bug protection."

Malachy claps his hands. "I think it's a fine idea for ya two to get away over the break. Ya both deserve some time to enjoy yourselves. But as much as I'd like to continue with talk of holidays on romantic islands, Garda Connell will be here soon, and I want ye to understand that he has some news."

"What kind of news?" Seamus asks.

"Not quite sure."

"Whatever it is," Nora says, "we can handle it." Her strength never ceases to amaze me.

As we clean up our dishes from dinner, there's a knock at the front door.

"Come in. Come on in, all of ya," Nora chimes good-naturedly.

Garda Connell, Caitlin O' Doughty, and a tall, slender man in a crisp white shirt and green bow tie sits on the sofa.

"Mac! I didn't know ya were comin' too." Malachy slaps the man on his back, a strong friendship evident between them as they join us in the sitting room.

"This is Mac McGarvey," Malachy says jovially, pointing at the bow-tied man with a pipe sticking out of his chest pocket.

"Mac," Nora explains, "is an ol' friend of Malachy's from school days. He's helped us more than once to save the farm now."

"Always my pleasure to help in any way I can." Mac dips his thinning dark-haired head at the Kavanaghs.

"He's here to help do just that today as well," Garda Connell says. He takes a deep breath before continuing. "I wanted to meet with ye to inform ya that we have a developin' plan in place to attempt to stop Nathair in whatever scheme they're plannin'."

We look at them expectantly.

"Nathair is a dangerous and unpredictable gang." Caitlin's voice trembles on the last word.

"I guess ya would know that, wouldn't ya?" Seamus' words cut like a knife, and she closes her eyes.

"Wait." Nora jumps in quickly. "We all need to remember that Caitlin's a victim here too."

"Nora's right." Malachy stands with her. "Caitlin is nothin' more than Nathair's pawn. She cannot be blamed."

"Very true," Garda Connell agrees. "Mac has looked o'er yer finances and any possibility of Nathair goin' after the farm. Luckily, he had the good sense to be proactive before the collapse of the bank."

"I tightened everything I could on your bank account and loan documents. I've ran them over and over again. I don't see Nathair bein' able to get to the farm, but that leaves," Mac glances at Seamus, *"Rocky Shore Fishin'* as a prime target. If they can't get the farm, it's goin' to be Seamus' business."

"So, how do we stop 'em?" Nora asks without a moment's hesitation.

"That brings us to our plan." Garda Connell gives Caitlin a weak smile. "Caitlin has agreed to help us, and that's not somethin' to be taken lightly. It takes a strong woman to take this on and risk everything. Caitlin will go undercover for us." He holds up a hand to stop the Kavanagh's protests. "No one needs to know she's with us. We will protect her."

"She'll help us catch the leader behind all of this?" Teagan looks both surprised and ashamed at the same time. Realizing Caitlin betrayed them was a hard blow, one Teagan has had a hard time getting over. I can see now though that Caitlin has won back some respect.

"I will do everything I can to do just that," Caitlin says with determination. "I don't know who's in charge, but I will try my best to find out."

"I believe ya will, dear, but it's awfully dangerous." Nora runs her fingers over her rosary beads, which are never far from her reach. "This is a personal vendetta, and whoever is behind it...well, we aren't sure how far they'll go."

"I will watch out for myself, and Garda Connell will be there for me too." She looks at him as if looking for assurance. "After the article in the Herald, security has been increased, and we're waitin' on their next move. The silence is unnerving,' so we're preparin' for the worst-case scenarios."

I suddenly remember that because of the response to my article, I never showed anyone the photo we found that day. "I have something to show everyone. I don't know if it will help at all, but Seamus and I found a photo at the shop."

I reach into my leather bag and pull the small photo frame out of a side pocket. "This is where we believe the answers will be found." I hand the photo to Garda Connell who examines it before handing it to Malachy.

The Kavanaghs look at the photo, and Nora gasps. "That's Maeve!"

"'Tis." Malachy looks over her shoulder.

Their shocked expressions make it clear that Michael and Maeve's relationship was unknown to them.

Seamus points to Maeve's hand in the photo. "We believe they were engaged."

Nora covers her mouth with a handkerchief. "Oh, dear."

Malachy leans forward, placing his elbows on his knees. "When they came to the farm that first night, they were speakin' about an awful feud and needing a place to stay. Never once did they mention Maeve and Michael bein' a couple."

"That's right." Nora looks out the window as if trying to remember the night. "They fit together so seamlessly. Never mentioned a word about how the feud started, and we left them to their own business."

"Their business included a trip to the bank." Mac's revelation has everyone looking to him for an explanation.

"What do ya mean to the bank? They were only with us a week or two. They had no need for the bank. If they were in trouble, we would have helped 'em." A line furrows between his eyebrows.

Mac wipes his forehead with the back of his hand. "They weren't the ones needin' help. Malachy, this was the same time that ya almost lost the farm?"

"Aye, we almost lost the farm, but we got the loan." Malachy throws his hands up in exasperation.

Mac looks between Malachy and Nora as if deciding how to proceed. "Ye got the loan because they put down a hefty deposit on the loan."

"Never!" Malachy stands, his face reddening.

"They didn't want ye to know, but James and Maeve found out about the farm's financial troubles, and they wanted to help. I gave 'em my word not to mention it to you." His eyes plead with Malachy to understand.

"Where would they have gotten the money for this?" Nora asks before realizing the truth. "They used the money from the shop. Michael must've bought them out."

Mac nods. "That's what they said. They paid in cash."

Malachy mumbles to himself while Nora closes her eyes.

"There's more," Mac says, looking like he'd rather be talking about anything else. "James and Maeve appeared spooked by somethin' or someone in town. They nearly ran away before I could ask about it. They were lookin' over their shoulder like expectin' someone to be followin' 'em. I deposited the money that day and drew up your loan agreement without further question."

Nora opens her eyes. "Dear souls. What could have spooked 'em so?"

Garda Connell closes his notepad. "I think that's where the answer to all of this may lie."

The kitchen door closes, and Cormac walks into the sitting room.

"Sorry to interrupt." He holds up a hand and turns to Malachy. "I didn't realize ya had company. Just wanted to tell ya Gandalf's shoes are mended. He should be good as gold now. Best to keep him off the soggy ground for a bit."

"Right ya are, we appreciate it. I hope the beast wasn't too hard on ya." Malachy shakes his hand.

"I wonder if Cormac has anything to add to our discussion." Seamus' tone is abrupt and raises a few eyebrows.

Does he still suspect Cormac may be a part of something? While I haven't disregarded the possibility, I can't find it in me to actually think he's involved. He's a part of the Kavanagh's family on the farm.

"What are ya talkin' about now?" Malachy asks.

"That day we were at the shop in Donegal, we saw Cormac walkin' back with his fish 'n chips. He was stopped by men on motorbikes, no doubt Nathair. They gave him somethin' in a brown paper bag."

All eyes are on Cormac.

"Ye think I'd be in with men like 'em?" He asks the room at large.

"What was in the bag?" Seamus demands. "Then we decide for ourselves, can't we?"

Cormac walks out of the room without a word. The kitchen door slams and there's silence.

"Do you think he's coming back?" Finn glances out of the back window.

"He'll be back." Nora leans back in her chair. "He's a good lad."

A couple minutes later, Cormac returns with the brown paper bag. He hands it to Seamus, anger in his eyes. "I know trouble when I see it. I have nothin' to do with those men."

Seamus empties the bag on the coffee table. A slip of

thick white paper with a drawing falls out, and a pristine green marble stone lands next to it.

"It's a rare form of Irish green." Cormac rubs the stone between his fingers. "Ya don't see a form of Connemara marble often, and when ya do, its price is too high to consider."

"Why would someone from Nathair give you this?" I ask.

"Don't know." He shrugs. "He asked me to take a look and see if I could put that image on it."

"Nathair's symbol." Teagan sits bedside the coffee table and examines the stone and drawing.

"I told him I had to go, and he said he'd be in touch. Creeped me out. I almost threw it right into the rubbish but couldn't make myself part with this stone that easily."

"Why didn't you say something to us?" I ask. "It doesn't make sense."

"When I got back to the shop, things were weird. It didn't feel like the right time."

He's right. Things were weird because we didn't know what he was doing. We were suspicious, and instead of just asking him about it, we assumed the worst and kept him at arm's length.

"I think we're missing a big point though," Teagan says. "These men know who you are."

"And," Garda Connell adds, "they know you're working for the Kavanaghs."

"Did they want Cormac to show us the stone?" Finn asks. "Maybe they're trying to tell us something."

"They won't scare us." Malachy pumps his fist.

Seamus continues to stare at Cormac. "I'm goin' to ask ya this one time, and ya'd better tell the truth. Are you in with Nathair?"

"Never." His eyes lock on Seamus.

After a long moment, the side of Seamus' lip quirks. "I believe ya."

Garda Connell paces the room. "I wish we knew if they were just testin' Cormac, tryin' to get him on their side, like Tommy, or if it's a message to us through Cormac."

The debate continues for another hour before Seamus drops me off at the cottage with more questions than answers.

"WHY ARE you looking for this woman?" Samara asks as we walk out of Professor Gaffney's lecture.

"She's important for this article I'm writing for the Herald." Maeve is technically connected to the article I wrote. I trust Samara, but I don't want to do anything else that might hinder the garda's investigation.

"I'll do what I can do to find her. Sophia is out of the office this week, so I should have some time to do a little side research."

"Thanks, Samara. You know that your research abilities are far beyond mine, especially with all of your connections now."

"Alright, I said I would help. No need to flatter me." She fluffs her short black curls. "Actually, go on and flatter me."

I laugh. "How about I buy you a coffee instead?"

She stares longingly at the student coffee shop at the end of the quad. "Deal!"

THE NEXT DAY I'm in the middle of writing an emotionally draining scene in my story when my phone rings. I'm about to ignore it when Samara's name flashes on the screen.

"Hi Samara. Are you working on your manuscript for Professor Gaffney?"

"Nope, I'm researching Maeve Sweeney."

I close my laptop. "Did you find something?"

"If by something you mean someone, then yes. I found her. It wasn't easy, but it appears she is living in the Ring of Kerry."

This means we may be able to talk to her and finally learn the truth of what happened between Michael and James.

"Listen, I have to get going," Samara whispers. "Do you have a pen to jot down the location?"

After writing Maeve's location in my notebook, I call Seamus. Looks like we're going to be taking another trip very soon.

"COME ON, JEMMA!" Seamus jostles the gear shift. "Ya can do it."

I put a hand over my mouth to suppress a laugh. We're inching up one of the winding hills along the Ring of Kerry and Seamus' old car is straining to reach the top.

We finally crest the hill, and Seamus gives the dashboard a pat. "Attagirl."

When we turn around the next bend, Seamus slows the car. "It's right up ahead."

He points to a charming white and terracotta cottage sitting on a hill, bordered by a gray stone fence. A bright peach-colored door sits between two open windows with matching shutters. Black window boxes hold cheerful yellow, blue, and red flowers. It's as welcoming a place as I've ever seen.

Seamus and I walk through the open gate and up the pathway lined with cheerful flowers on each side. A coiled brown doormat sits just before the door, and a white flower wreath hangs above a brass door knocker. As I reach for the knocker, the door slides open, and a slight woman with warm hazel eyes appears. Her fair skin is lightly lined with wrinkles and her shoulder-length red curls are streaked with gray. Deep laugh lines hug her eyes and thin mouth.

"Can I help ye?" She puts a hand on the large blue-gray terrier standing by her side.

"Hi, I'm Kayleigh O'Reilly, and this is Seamus Murphy. We're looking for Maeve Sweeney."

"Hmm," she murmurs. "And what do you need with this Maeve Sweeney?"

"We're not here for any harm." Seamus holds his hand over his heart, much like Nora. "We just wanted to speak with her about something she might be able to help us with."

"And what do ye need help with?"

Maeve Sweeney seems like a woman who appreciates honesty, and I decide to be straight with her. "Ms. Sweeney," I say, looking her in the eye, "we need to know what happened to *O'Doherty and Brannan's Pot o' Gold*. You are our last hope in stopping something horrible from happening in Cloverdale."

Surprise and respect shine in her eyes. "I think ye better come on in. Looks like we have a lot to talk about."

CHAPTER ELEVEN

Maeve offers us tea from a brass tea tray in her sitting room. I sip the black tea and take in the artwork on the walls. There are watercolor landscapes of the countryside, pen and ink portraits, and an intricate metal trinity knot. A remarkable clay bust of what appears to be her dog sits in the center of the mahogany side table.

Glass blown trinket bowls and vases are sitting on various surfaces about the room. A sapphire blue vase catches my eye. It's rounded base and fluted stem resembles a wave rising from the sea.

"Michael and I used to love blowing glass," she says, following my gaze. "Each of our creations is a memory from our time together."

"They're lovely, Ms. Sweeney," I say.

"Please call me Maeve." She continues to look at the glass vase, seemingly lost in a memory. "Every day was an adventure with Michael."

"I'm sure ya miss him very much." Seamus is gentle with his words.

"Everyday. He was the love of my life. But life continues.

Michael wouldn't want me to be mopin' 'round. 'Keep the flowers growing,' he'd say." She smiles at this. "I've always loved my flowers, and he would call them a work of art, sayin' no greater artist ever lived."

The love between them is clear. "I'm sorry. I'm sure it's so painful to lose the love of your life."

"'Tis. But I know I will see him again. It's not truly the end."

Her dog appears to notice her owner is feeling nostalgic and places her head in Maeve's lap.

"Your dog is beautiful. What breed is she?" I ask.

"Annie's a good girl." She smooths the tuffs of ringed hair by the dog's brown eyes. "She's a Kerry Blue Terrier. You can pet her if ya'd like. She's a mighty friendly one."

I reach out and run my hand over her soft coat. "I bet Colonel would love to run with Annie."

"Colonel?" she asks.

"Kayleigh's mess of an Irish wolfhound," Seamus says, sounding proud of the dog despite his words.

"Aw, you love him." I shoot him a teasing smile.

He huffs. "I wouldn't go that far."

"A dog can be a girl's best defender." Maeve looks lovingly at Annie. "And they sure are good company. It can get lonely out here by myself without her."

There's a lull in the conversation, and a I take the opportunity to ask Maeve about the shop. "Maeve, we came here today to talk to you about *O'Doherty and Brannan's Pot o' Gold*."

She settles back into the chair cushions. "I knew I'd have to talk about it one day."

Seamus and I fill her in on everything we know so far and the implications to the Kavanagh's farm, Seamus' fishing business, and Cloverdale.

"Oh, dear. I'm sorry to hear of this affecting your family." She twists a gold wedding band around her left ring finger.

"You don't doubt all of this is Nathair?" Seamus asks.

She closes her eyes tightly before opening them again. "Nathair is capable of much harm. They are personal in their attacks. My life would have been very different if not for them."

Her description of Nathair does nothing to ease my mind about our current situation. "How so?" I ask.

"They stole my first love away from me and broke what I thought was an unbreakable friendship." She gets a faraway look in her eyes. "It's hard for me to revisit that time."

I walk over to her chair and sit in front of her. "I can only image how that feels." I take the photo out of my bag. "We found this in the shop. I think you should have it."

She takes the photo from me. "Oh, my heart." She covers her mouth with her hand. "It seems like only yesterday."

"What happened, Maeve?" I ask gently.

She takes a deep breath before releasing it slowly. "As a child, my homelife was not what it should've been. The O'Dougherty's took me in. They treated me like one of the family."

She puts the photo on the arm of the chair and strokes Annie's ears. "Michael's sister Erin was my dearest friend. We did everythin' together as in our young days. As we grew older, and with me being a couple years older than Erin, I began havin' feelin's for Michael, and he felt the same way back then. Michael and I were the ones spendin' all of our time together. I believe Erin felt left out, and I see now how she'd feel that way. At the time though, I was fallin' deeply in love and didn't realize. When Michael proposed I didn't hesi-tate to say yes."

After a few moments, I ask, "Is it because of Erin that you two broke it off?"

A sadness fills her eyes. "It wasn't Erin. I think o'er time, things would have been better. I was goin' to be her sister, after all. It's what we had always wanted. There's someone else who came between us."

Could James have stolen his best friend's fiancée? The idea doesn't sit right with me, and I can't hold back my opinion. "I can't see how James could have broken you two up."

She gives a sad chuckle. "Oh, it wasn't James. He had a heart of gold and was as loyal as any man can be."

"Was it Nathair?" Seamus' question has me holding my breath.

"Aye," she says, "it was. Well, their influence anyway. It was Michael who made the decision for himself."

"How do you mean?" I take a sip of tea, hoping it will soothe my stomach.

"Michael fell in with the wrong fellas. He started goin' out with 'em every night, leavin' me alone and wonderin' why he was choosin' 'em over me. He was drinkin' heavily in those days and denied it, but I know there was harder stuff too. He didn't show for work at the shop so many times that James confronted him, and Michael blew up sayin' to get out of his life."

Maeve looks at the photo again. "He was no longer the Michael that I knew and loved. Nathair destroyed him. Our relationship fell apart. The shop was headin' in a bad direction. James and I were left to pick up the pieces of our shattered lives."

Seamus leans forward. "We saw financial documents at the shop, and everythin' looked good. How did they stay afloat?"

"James. He covered for Michael until one day they got into a brawl o'er ownership. Michael wanted to have Nathair buy into the shop as partial owner. He had it in his mind that they were his real mates—the ones who would make all of his dreams come true. And Michael was a dreamer if there ever was one. James was the practical one. He did not trust

Nathair or Michael anymore. It hurt him so. He lost his best friend and his own dream of runnin' the shop all at once. He closed the shop to prevent it becomin' something he couldn't bear to see. He knew no good could come of a partnership with Nathair."

"I assume Michael didn't take it well?" Seamus asks.

"He was furious. I tried to help him see what was goin' on, but he was a lost soul at that point. He broke off our engagement sayin' I was a trader just like James. They dissolved the contract for the shop, and James took his part of the money and left for Cloverdale with me in tow. I had nowhere else to go. The only family I had left was the O'Doughertys, and they couldn't see what was happenin' with Michael. When they found out that he called off the engagement, they blamed me sayin' I was two-timing him with James. None of it was true."

"You had nowhere else left to go." Maeve was young and scared and must have felt completely alone. "And James was the only one who knew the truth."

"We were in it together. We went to the Kavanagh's farm. James said they would help us, and it was the God's honest truth. Malachy and Nora were nothin' but kind and generous to us."

"They took me in when my parents passed too. I would've been lost without 'em." Seamus tells her. "Mac McGarvey told us about the day ye went to the bank. He didn't want to mind ya, he's a good man and kept the secret all of these years, but we need all the help we can get to stop Nathair. There's too much riding on this to keep any secrets."

"Aye, " she says in acknowledgement. "I prayed my heart out that it would all end back then. Knowin' it's still goin' on, and to the finest people, breaks my heart all o'er again." She shakes her head. "I don't blame him. When we learned of the Kavanagh's financial problems with the farm, we wanted to help 'em just as they had helped give us shelter and privacy. They never questioned us or prodded into our past, just accepted us as we were. For that, I will be forever grateful."

"I know the feelin'," Seamus agrees. "Many of us do."

"Mac mentioned," I say, "that it appeared you two were spooked by something in the town."

"I'll never forget that day we went into town. We met with Mac at the bank, and we used part of the money from the shop as the down payment. It wasn't much, but it was enough for Mac to be able to draw up a new loan for 'em. He asked us if we wanted to get a pint at the pub, and we agreed. It had been a long time since we'd had anything to celebrate. And helping the Kavanaghs was a grand reason to celebrate. On our way, we spotted someone that threw us. He had no reason to be there unless he was lookin' for us."

"Was it someone from Nathair?" I ask, hoping to finally make a connection between Nathair and their presence in Cloverdale.

"Aye. James and Michael had an assistant at the shop. He went by the name of Pat, but I never knew his last name or much about him. He was a hard worker and a natural with the metalwork. When things started gettin' bad for Michael, Pat followed right along. He always looked up to Michael. We saw him in the street talkin' to another man, and we knew he was there lookin' for us. We knew in that moment that it wouldn't be safe to stay in Cloverdale. We left not long after, and I'm sorry to say that I haven't been to the town since that day. Even after all these years, I prefer to stay low. I enjoy the peace and privacy the country affords. Ye are the first people to come see me in many years."

I can almost see the truth registering in her mind. If we could find her, then Nathair could too. She continues, "If Nathair is rising as ye say, nowhere will be safe anymore."

I give her a hopeful smile. "Unless we stop them."

As Seamus and I drive back to Brigid's Crossing, I take in the views of the mountain peaks and sheep covered fields.

"Ya were somethin' to watch in there." Seamus glances at me as he turns onto another long and winding road.

"What do you mean?"

"It was like watchin' a story come to life. Ya have a way about ya that helps people to open up."

I've always been what I consider a good listener, but could it really have the impact that Seamus is implying? "Maybe that's why I'm a reporter."

He scrunches his nose in what resembles a grimace. "Maybe, but that was more than reportin' in there. That was connection. Ya're a people person, Kayleigh. Ya naturally understand and relate to people and their experiences in a way that ya don't see often."

"Teagan's joked about me changing majors for counseling," I say, dismissing the idea with a wave of my hand.

"I don't think she was jokin'. I've known Teagan for a while, and I don't hear many jokes from her, but she is brilliantly observant."

I have considered the idea before, but I can't imagine giving up writing. "If there was a way to combine counseling and writing, that would be a dream."

"I'd say," he agrees.

As we drive to Brigid's Crossing, I imagine a life where my dreams could become a reality.

When we arrive at the farm, everyone is waiting for Garda Connell to arrive. Seamus, Finn, Teagan, and Cormac go out into the barn with Malachy to see about a new Connemara pony they just rescued. We stopped by the cottage on the way to pick up Colonel, and he happily joins them, eager for the fun and adventure that the fresh air and farm animals provide. I choose to stay inside with Nora as she sews in the corner chair.

"That's beautiful." I sit on the loveseat adjacent to her.

"It's no small thing to sew for the Lord." She fingers the edges of the white lace.

"What are you making?"

"This is a chapel veil for little Shannon. She's been admirin' her mama's and wanted one of her own, so I told her I'd make her one just as lovely as she."

Shannon is a little girl with cerebral palsy who participates in Teagan and Finn's equine-assisted therapy program. "I'm sure she'll love it."

"I do hope so. As a sign of humanity and beauty, the chapel veil is a treasured tradition in our town."

I find myself drawn to the veil and the desire to learn more. "I've seen them occasionally at home, but never knew the reason behind wearing one."

"The veil helps to direct out thoughts, intentions, and desires to Jesus. Wearing one is a beautiful act of imitation of our Lady, the Blessed Virgin Mary, who always points us to her son. It may be an outward symbol, but it's inside where there's a humblin' of spirit. When you wear a veil, yer whole self is a form of worship." She reaches into her fabric case and pulls out a cream-colored veil. "Try this on an see for yerself."

I place the delicate lace over my head and fasten the clip into place. The lace flows around the sides of my face and drapes back onto my shoulders. A feeling of reverence descends. "Nora, it's lovely."

She smiles. "This one is yours."

"Oh, no," I say quickly, "It's too much."

"Oh, blarney! I made it and have been waitin' for the person it belongs too. Seein' ya now, I know ya're that girl."

I remove the veil and smooth the lace in my hands. "Thank you, Nora. I will treasure this." I place the veil in the zippered compartment of my bag.

"I know ya will, dear." She searches the large tufted sewing box when I catch a glint.

"Nora, that ring looks identical to the one from the photo with Michael and Maeve." I point to the gold ring.

Nora pushes her reading glasses back up her nose. "Oh, dear." She lifts the ring from among the pins and loose pieces of thread. "I had forgotten about this ring. It's comin' back to me now. I found it in the cottage years ago. Never knew who it belonged to, so I kept it in case I discovered the owner one day."

She hands me the ring, and I pull the photo out of my bag. I compare the bright sapphire stone sitting in a granite inlay. The gold band is scratched but has maintained its luster. "It's Maeve's ring."

And now I know I need to make another trip to the Ring of Kerry.

A LITTLE WHILE LATER, Garda Connell arrives, and we are all settled back into the sitting room. Seamus and I fill everyone in on our time with Maeve. After agreeing that she is a strong ally and potentially holds the key to finding Nathair's connection with Cloverdale, the conversation redirects to a person who knows more than she's willing to share—Teagan and Finn's old mentor from the summer scholars' program, Fiona Kelly.

Garda Connell has his notepad open to review his notes. "While Fiona is serving her time in prison, she's not cooperating with the inquiry. I have no doubt she's still an active part of Nathair's plan, though I'm not sure how she fits in yet."

Teagan shifts in her seat next to me on the sofa. "How can she be active while in jail? Someone must be helping her."

"We believe that's the case." Garda Connell returns his notepad to his pocket.

"What can we do to discover who it is?" Finn asks.

"I'm afraid nothin' at this point." He looks around the room. "I wish there was, mind ya, but we must wait and see."

Teagan slouches back into the sofa cushion. "Unfortunately, that's not something I'm good at."

I give her hand a sympathetic squeeze. "I know it's hard, but it can't be long before someone offers up a clue."

"I don't know." Cormac interjects. "If Nathair is connected to the community in some way, it means someone knows, but they're stayin' quiet."

"That is an awful truth," Malachy agrees.

Garda Connell puts his cap on and makes his way to the front door. "It's a truth that's hard to come to terms with, but one that requires our awareness. We don't know who we can trust."

I consider the community of Cloverdale. The one thing that stands out is their loyalty to each other.

Is it possible that someone from the town is hiding a dark secret?

CHAPTER TWELVE

A few weeks later, there is a knock on the cottage door. When I open it, Seamus stands there with a huge grin on his face.

"Is there good news?" I ask, thinking about the lunch meeting he had earlier in the day with Malachy and Garda Connell.

His smile loses some of its brilliance. "No news yet. Things are still quiet, and no new leads either." He shifts on his feet. "But I have other news."

I motion for him to come in. "What kind of news?"

He sits at the kitchen table while I put the kettle on the stove. "Remember when I told ya about my meetin' with Jackson's? They've offered me a contract."

An unease stirs within me. "Oh."

Seamus was approached by Jackson's Seafood as a potential supplier of fish. Their interest is unusual given they are such a large company, and Seamus' business is just starting off. There's no personal connection between them, and I wonder how they even heard of Seamus and *Rocky Shore Fishing*.

He looks at me expectantly, and I try again. "That's good."

Maybe it's too good to be true. I take the kettle from the stove and add the black tea bags.

"That's it?" His grin fades. "They're the big time, Kayleigh. To have a partnership with Jackson's would be the best thing for my business. It would take it to the next level. All of Ireland would know of us."

I pour us each a cup of the tea and sit with Seamus at the table.

"It does sound amazing, but where is their interest coming from? We know Nathair is trying to get to you and the Kavanaghs, and it seems suspicious to me. What if Nathair is behind this? If you sign something with them, they could potentially take everything away from you."

"But they're not. Jackson's is legit." He takes too big of a sip of the hot tea and curses. "I thought ya'd be happy for me."

"I am. It just doesn't feel right."

I reach for him, but he stands and runs a hand through his hair. "Ah, yer back to goin' off feelin's again?"

The barb strikes. I lower my teacup to the table. "I suppose I am."

"I thought that didn't work in the past? I'm tryin' to do right and make somethin' of myself."

I know how much he wants this partnership. It would provide the success he so longs for, but how can I help him see that success doesn't have to come in the form of some big-name company, but can be found in a small town like Cloverdale?

I walk over to him. "Do you really want to supply the big chains and lose business in the small shops—shops that are run by families you've known your whole life?"

"This is my big break. To partner with a big chain like Jackson's would put me in a whole different level in business and my life."

What's wrong with his life now? "It's a great opportunity for you. I just want you to make sure it will make you happy."

His softens at this. "Listen, I want to stay in Cloverdale—it's home. I just don't want to miss out on this and regret it later."

"I think you could regret it either way. And I don't say it to try to influence your decision, but will you please talk with the Kavanaghs and Garda Connell."

He leans against the wall. "It couldn't hurt to run it by 'em."

I run my hand down his arm. "I think that would be good."

As much as I don't like dampening his joy, I can't shake the twinge of apprehension that something's just not right.

A WEEK later I'm working on my story for the *Saints and Scholar's* program when my phone rings.

"Hello?" I answer without looking at the name.

"Kayleigh?"

"Fiadh, what's wrong?" I close my laptop when I hear her crying.

"Da's no longer with the paper." She blows her nose.

"What do you mean?" Why would Mr. Dempsey leave the paper?

"The paper has been bought out. Da said he had no choice but to sign it away."

No choice? Every time I've seen Mr. Dempsey I'm left with the feeling that the paper would continue to be a cornerstone in the community for years to come. "I didn't know your dad was even thinking about selling the paper."

"He wasn't. It's been in our family for generations. He was goin' to pass it on to me when the time was right," she sobs.

It doesn't make any sense. "If your dad loves the paper, why did he sell it?"

Fiadh sniffles. "Kayleigh, Da is scared. I don't know why, but he is."

Dread creeps in. "I'm so sorry, Fiadh." I almost don't want to ask the next question, but I force myself to. "Do you know who the buyer is?"

She blows her nose. "Da said a fellow at the university."

My breath catches in my chest. "Did he say his name?" I ask, trying to maintain composure.

"Aye. Mr. Banwell."

AFTER I END the call with Fiadh, I call Teagan and tell her everything. I release all of my pent-up emotions about Seamus and the Jackson's deal and the shocking buyout of the Cloverdale Herald.

She's quiet as she takes it all in, and I give her time to respond. Having a sister means you know them better than anyone else, and when Teagan is quiet like this, it means she is deep in thought. When she is still silent a few minutes later, I fear there's more I don't know. "Teagan, what's going on?"

I hear movement in the background and know she's up and pacing now. "Garda Connell stopped by earlier. Fiona's escaped from prison."

I gasp. "How?"

"No one knows, but between the bank, her disappearance, this Jackson's thing, and now the newspaper, I think everything's about to come to a head."

MY CONVERSATION with Teagan leaves me unsettled and worried about Seamus that I can't just sit by and wait for something horrible to happen. I dial the number for Jackson's and pray that everything is as up-front as Seamus hopes.

"Jackson's, how can I help ya?" The female voice is clipped, as if she's in the middle of something.

"Hi. I'm doing research about the fishing industry for the university, and I'm hoping to speak with someone about the business side of Jackson's."

"I'll connect you with our communications manager. Please hold."

There's a clicking of lines before a woman's voice comes on the line. "This is Janet speaking."

"Hi. I'm doing research about the fishing industry for Emerald Isle University and would love to learn more about Jackson's." I force my voice to remain unsuspecting.

"I only have a few minutes, but I can give ya a quick breakdown."

"Thank you. I really appreciate your time." I've learned that when Rory Jackson began the business, he was a small-town fisherman. The company has grown so much over the past decade. "How does he still care for small town businesses being a corporate organization?" I ask.

She sighs. "Rory Jackson is as smart and kind a businessman as ye'll ever find. We will all miss him dearly."

"What do you mean?" I tighten my grip on my pencil as I wait for her answer.

"Rory Jackson no longer owns Jackson's."

My heart begins to race. "Is that so? Who is the new owner?" I hold my breath.

"Mr. Colin Banwell is the new owner of Jackson's."

"HE'S TAKING OVER EVERYTHING." Teagan paces back and forth across the cottage a few hours later.

Colonel whimpers and lays his head on his paws. He must sense the tension in the room.

"Can't believe I almost went into business with them." Seamus shakes his head and looks miserable.

"You couldn't have known." I try to soothe him.

"But ya did." He takes my hand between his. "I could've lost it all if it weren't for ya." He looks at me with a mixture of gratitude and something deeper.

I hold his gaze. "I'm glad I could help."

"Malachy's meeting with Garda Connell now, and maybe they can tell us more soon." Teagan's nervous energy seems to radiate off of her.

Finn leans back in the rocking chair. "I can't believe that Banwell is the leader behind all of this. He has to be the front man."

Finn has a point, and it's one I've considered as well. "I was thinking about that too. Fiadh said Mr. Dempsey had no choice but to sign the papers. Why no choice?"

"Nathair is threatening them." Teagan stops pacing. "They have to be, or why else would everyone be falling to them?"

"Threatening their businesses?" I ask.

"Maybe." Teagan looks skeptical. "But, they're already losing their businesses. Would they have signed for money alone, or is there something else?"

I turn to Seamus this time. He might be feeling disappointed about Jackson's right now, but no one knows the people of Cloverdale better than him. "What's something the business owners love more than money?"

"The town." He leaves no room for debating this. "People 'round here take pride in their work and pride in our traditions."

I've seen it in Seamus' business, in the Kavanagh's farm,

and even with Teagan and Finn's program. The town is family. It's true what we've been hearing all along—this is a personal vendetta.

"They're planning on taking over the whole town," I say, wishing the words to be untrue.

A COUPLE OF DAYS LATER, I stand outside the Emerald Isle newspaper office waiting for Samara. After fifteen minutes, she comes out the door looking more than a bit frazzled.

"What's going on?" I ask.

She wipes her forehead with the back of the sleeve of her red Aran sweater. "The whole team is in a frenzy. News just broke about a previous employee of Emerald Isle, and there's a rush to get all the details. I'm sorry, but I'm not going to be able to get dinner together. Can we reschedule?"

"Of course." I glance around to make sure no one can overhear. "Is it something about Mr. Banwell?"

She shakes her head. "Fiona Kelly."

"Did they find her?" My heart leaps at the thought that the garda may have captured Fiona.

"Yes." She looks around again before turning back to me. "She's dead."

AN HOUR later I'm in Teagan's dorm room with her and Finn.

"This is bad." Teagan is pacing the small space. "Ryan is going to lose it."

"We don't know that," Finn interjects, but he doesn't sound like he believes what he's saying any more than we do. "Caitlin doesn't know anything concrete."

Caitlin has been in touch with Garda Connell, and

everyone is on edge because she warned that Nathair has a plan in place, though she doesn't know what it is. After news of Fiona's death, Ryan is not following by this plan, and she fears he may do something without Nathair's governing.

"Do they know how she died?" I ask, wishing Samara had more details to share.

"They are calling it a likely homicide because of the suspicious nature of her body." Finn reaches out a hand and pulls Teagan next to him. "It's going to be okay."

She slides onto the bed next to him. "I hope you're right. I just have a bad feeling."

"So, what was the suspicious nature of her death?" I ask.

"She was found floating in the Dublin Bay," Teagan tells me. "There was blunt force trauma to her head."

"It could have been an accident. She may have slipped and fallen on a dock. Or she could've—" Finn cuts off when he catches our looks.

"Come on, Finn, of course it wasn't an accident." Teagan lays her head on Finn's shoulder. "Who could've done it? And why dump her body in the bay? Whoever it was must have known her body would surface quickly."

"Maybe that's what they wanted." Teagan and Finn look at me. "If it seems unlikely to be an accident, I doubt the placement of her body is an accident either."

Teagan stands up and begins pacing again. I can practically see her mind working through the details. "You're right. It seems so obvious now."

"Yeah, I agree, but we still don't know who killed Fiona."

Hearing it out loud sends a ripple of nerves through me. Fiona was killed. It wasn't an accident but rather a deliberate action. And the killer is still loose.

CHAPTER THIRTEEN

The next morning I try to work on my history assignment, but thoughts of Nathair and Seamus keep entering my mind. If Ryan is on the brink of a breakdown, wouldn't Seamus be a likely target? Garda Connell and the Kavanaghs are already worried about Seamus' business, but what if they go after him? I don't know if it's the reporter instinct, but there's a feeling that something is about to break loose. The thought of losing him makes my stomach turn.

I dial Seamus' number, hoping that talking with him will ease my nerves, but there's no answer. Unable to sit still for another minute, I grab my coat and Colonel's leash.

"Come on, boy. We're going to the docks."

Colonel and I hop off the trolley and make the short walk to the docks. The rain is more of a mist than the soaking downpour of earlier.

Colonel pads along ahead of me, ears perked happily, knowing the way to the boat. He gives two sharp, excited yips before running across the long planked dock to *Crossways*. He wags his tail and whines as he waits for me to catch up with him.

"Go on," I tell him, and he leaps onto the boat.

The sight of Seamus soothes my worried heart. He's standing at the bow of the boat with his back to us, looking out into the bay. I step onto the boat and steady myself with the rail. It's like he's searching for an answer in the sea.

I walk over next to him. "The sea is beautiful."

He jumps at my voice. "Kayleigh, I didn't see ya there." His smile is forced.

"What's wrong?" The feeling of dread returns.

His lips thin as he looks back out to sea. "Had some bad news this mornin'." He leans his elbows against the railing. "Keefe, the new manager over at O'Callahan's Pub, called to cancel our partnership." His tone is matter-of-fact. The clenching of his jaw muscle is the only sign of emotion.

"Why?" I lay my hand on his arm. Seamus worked at O'Callahan's for years. He's been their fish and seafood provider the whole time. What could cause them to break such a strong partnership?

He stares at the waves lapping against the side pier. "Food poisoning."

The urge to defend him is immediate. "It can't be your fish. You're so careful about everything."

He shrugs as if he's completely given up. "Food poisoning is enough to shut down a business like mine. May never come back after a blow like this, but that's only a drop in the bucket to what happened to those people."

"It's Nathair." My blood is pumping. "I know it. They're doing this to put you out of business."

He runs a hand through his thick dark hair. "Aye. I believe ya may be right." Sadness floods his eyes. The fight that I would expect from him is unnervingly absent. "Nothin' to be done now."

I can't let him give up now. "There's plenty to be done! They need to be held accountable for what they did. We need to—"

"Kayleigh, stop." Seamus closes his eyes for a moment. "People got sick. Ya hear me? They could've died. Fiona is dead. This is not a game. We can't be playing detective with people's lives. It's not a story in a book. It's real life."

"I know it's not a story!" I counter defensively. "And what do you mean 'playing detective?' Seamus, you know as well as me, actually more than me, what Nathair is capable of doing. How can you push that aside?"

Anger flashes in his eyes now. "I'm not pushin' anythin' aside. I'm bein' realistic. My business is ruined. Who's goin' to buy from me now? And even if they would, I can't take a chance of somethin' like this happenin' again. It's too big of a risk."

Realistic is not a word I would have ever used to describe Seamus. But as deflating as it is to hear, there is truth in what he's saying. Nathair will keep doing this until Seamus backs away from *Rocky Shore Fishing.* They know he would not put people's lives in danger. But, if he gives in, we're letting them win. "We can't give in to evil. And that's what Nathair is— evil."

He looks intently at me now, some of that Seamus passion flashing in the depths of his eyes. It urges me to continue. I need him to be the fighter I know he is. "You are not alone in this. You have your family and the town behind you. You have friends, *real* friends." My voice cracks on the last word. "Friends who believe in you and would never leave you on your own during this. You can't give up. Seamus, your passion is what made me fall in love with you."

Did I just tell Seamus that I love him? His stricken

expression confirms it. And from the looks of it, it wasn't the right thing to say.

The boat sways, and I grasp the rail. "I don't know why I said that."

I meet his eyes, and I want nothing more than to draw him close. I'm not sure when it happened, but I've fallen completely and utterly in love with Seamus Murphy.

"No, I do know." My courage builds. "I'm in love with you."

His mouth hangs open slightly, but no words come out. I send up a silent prayer that his answer is the one I long for.

But, it's a prayer left unanswered.

The water lapping against the boat is the only sound. I finally turn away from him and walk to the back of the boat. A quick pat of my leg calls Colonel to me as I step onto the dock. Colonel leaps up next to me, and we walk down the dock together. I hold my head high, just like I did that day months earlier leaving Magnolia's Cafe. A single tear rolls down my cheek as I feel Seamus watching me leave.

I sit on the wooden bench at the trolley stop, Colonel laying at my feet. His soft snoring rumbles against my ankle boot.

Where did it all go wrong?

The connection between me and Seamus is strong. There's no denying it. Although, I have been wrong about that in the past. If I had gotten my relationship with Chris so completely wrong, could I be wrong about Seamus as well?

I pull out my phone and click the call button for our sisters' video chat. As soon as I see Teagan and Ashling's faces, I begin telling them everything.

"Wait," Teagan says, narrowing her eyes. "What happened with Seamus and *Rocky Shore Fishing*?"

I realize that my earlier declaration of love overshadowed the significance of what Seamus revealed. I go on to explain the situation, and my sisters have very different reactions.

"Oh, if I were there, I'd give them a piece of my mind!" Ashling is visibly angry. "I'm so glad everyone is okay, but it's not right to let Seamus take the blame for this."

Hearing Ashling's reaction makes me feel justified in my own reaction to the news. People often assume that Teagan and I are the most alike. And they wouldn't necessarily be wrong, but while my emotional tendencies can drive Ashling crazy, there's a strong connection between us too. Maybe it's our artistic sides that pull us closer—my writing and her art. I think in some way we've both always looked up to Teagan, who seems to have everything together. I know that no matter whatever happens, my sisters will always be at my side.

"Teagan, what do you think?" I ask, hoping she's formulating a plan of action.

She bites her lower lip. "I think that we should wait and see what happens."

Ashling gapes at her. "You mean, do nothing? Are you crazy?"

I have to admit that I'm thinking the same thing.

"Well," Teagan purses her lips, "not do *nothing*, but I'm not sure a big action is the right decision right now."

"Something has to be done!" I can't hold back anymore. Why are Seamus and Teagan just giving up?

"Kayleigh," Teagan warns, "you can't let your emotions take over. You have to think logically about this."

"Right. I forgot. I don't know anything about real life." My tone is snippy, and I catch the surprise on their faces.

"That's not what I'm saying at all," Teagan reassures. "Everyone's emotions are high right now. There's a lot going on with Nathair, and with you and Seamus, Kayleigh. I think we should just step back for a little bit and—"

"No," I say definitively. "We don't need time. We need action! What we need is some grand gesture to stop all of this."

They are both looking at me with wide eyes now. Every good story has a grand gesture. This is no different.

"Kayleigh, what are you thinking of doing?" Teagan's tone is slow and deliberate. "Please don't do anything without talking to us this time."

Her words sting. I know she's referring to the mistake with the news article. "This is different."

"Maybe," Teagan agrees, "but let's think about it more before we do anything. And Seamus had a big blow. It's obvious he loves you too. He just needs time too."

The trolley pulls up to the stop, and as I'm about to step onto the platform, a message pops up on my phone from Seamus.

Can you meet me at the boat? We need to talk.

"I have to go," I say quickly, turning from the trolley. "Seamus just texted me about needing to talk."

"Where are you going?" Ashling asks, confusion evident in her expression.

"Back to his boat."

"Kayleigh, you should wait," Teagan warns. "Something doesn't seem right."

"I have to go. I'll call you back later," I say, before ending the call.

Without another thought, Colonel and I walk back towards the docks.

WHEN WE REACH the main planked dock, Colonel stops and growls at the shadowed boats bobbing in the sunset. I pull on his leash, but he won't budge.

"Colonel," I urge, "we need to go see Seamus."

He doesn't react. The docks are eerily quiet.

"Let's go back to the trolley stop and call Seamus," I tell Colonel, trying to push aside the growing fear.

Colonel spins around and leaps at movement to my side. A large dirty hand covers my mouth, muffling my scream.

"Don't be tryin' anythin'." A deep voice whispers in my ear as Colonel's barks are frantic and strained.

His warm breath reeks of alcohol. He pulls me onto a nearby boat, and I watch through bleary eyes the dock disappearing as we descend the narrow steps to the cabin underneath.

He pushes me into a dark closet, and I fall onto the hard, damp wooden floor. The sound of a lock is the last thing I hear before everything goes dark.

CHAPTER FOURTEEN

A light flickers through the opening of the door, creating a halo effect in the dimness. I roll over, my elbow scraping against a sharp nail jutting out from the wooden floor.

"Ow." I groan and press my hand over the open wound as blood trickles around my fingers.

"Are you okay?"

I gasp. "Seamus?"

"Aye." He tears off a piece of his cotton undershirt and applies pressure to my cut. "Ya've been out for a while."

"I don't understand. What are you doing here?"

I rub my head as if trying to dislodge the cobwebs. Images flash through my muddled mind—me and Seamus on his boat, my confession, the call with my sisters, the eerily quiet dock, the grungy hand over my mouth, Colonel's barking. Oh, Colonel. What happened to him?

"I could ask ya the same thing."

I remember his text message. "I got your message. That's why I came back to the dock."

He runs a hand through his hair. "I didn't send ya a message, Kayleigh."

My stomach sinks. "You didn't want to talk?" The pain of knowing this numbs my throbbing elbow.

"I didn't send ya a message, but I did want to talk. I was on my way to the cottage to talk with ya about everythin', but then Teagan called. She was worried about ya and the message ya got. I rushed back down to the dock, and he was waitin' for me."

The scent memory of the man's breath turns my stomach. "Who was waiting?"

"Ryan."

I was such a fool. Why didn't I listen to Teagan? Even Ashling looked confused at the text. Was my heart so hopeful at the sight of the message that I threw away all sense and reason? I thought I had grown so much since being in Ireland, but it turns out I'm still making the same mistakes I was before.

I close my eyes, welcoming the darkness. "It's all my fault."

"No," Seamus says quickly, pulling me even closer. "It was me who got ya into this in the first place. Nathair knows. They have eyes everywhere, and they can see plainly my feelin's for you, even if I might stumble understandin' 'em myself. They can ruin my business and livelihood, that would hurt me, but they know I would go mad if I ever lost ya."

Even in the dim light he must see the questions in my eyes as I look into his. "I'm so sorry about earlier, Kayleigh."

"You don't have to be sorry." Seamus doesn't owe me anything. I love Seamus, and there's no denying that. Even if he doesn't feel the same way, I want him to be a part of my life.

"No, but I am. I was an eejit! When ya told me that ya

love me, I didn't know what to say. I know, me without words, it's unheard of."

Despite the gravity of the conversation, I laugh.

"It wasn't because I don't feel the same way about ya, 'cause I do. After everythin' with my business, I didn't want ya involved with any of this anymore, and I thought that by puttin' some distance between us, Nathair might leave ya be. I should've known better."

My heart swells. This man, so strong and good and kind, not only loves me but was trying to protect me.

Instead of words, I kiss him with all the words I'm not saying. It's as if the whole world fades away, and it's only me and Seamus.

"Isn't love grand?" A man with a broken nose and bandaged eye stares at us through the porthole window.

Seamus clenches his fists. "Ryan." The name is spat out like a curse word.

Ryan's lips curl into a wicked smile. He pulls the door open slowly and points a handgun at us. "How's it feel to be in love, Seamus?"

Seamus stares back at him but doesn't say anything.

Ryan looks up with a feigned thoughtful gesture. "Is it better to have loved and lost or...come on, Seamus, you know the rest."

When Seamus doesn't say anything, Ryan cocks the trigger. His sinister grin tells me that he'd love nothing more than to pull it.

"Or to never have loved at all." I finish the Shakespeare quote, unwilling to allow him to play Seamus like this.

Ryan looks at me like he's seeing me for the first time. "Aye, that's right. Yer both writers. How nice. I bet ya love reciting poetry with our boy here, don't ya?"

"What do you want with us?" I ask, more boldly than I feel.

When he laughs, I raise my voice. "You won't get away with this."

He laughs even louder, the sound mimicking that of a deranged clown. "I see what ya see in her, mate. She's quite the beauty and has a feisty side, just like my Fiona...." The muscle along his jaw clenches, and his breathing becomes more rapid. "But, I lost her, didn't I?" Hate fills his eyes—eyes pointed right at Seamus.

"Let Kayleigh go. I'm the one ya want." Seamus holds up his hands in surrender, but I see the fight coming back to him.

Ryan steps forward, leaving a small gap between him and the door. I catch Seamus' eye and the almost nonexistent nod he makes towards the door. I inch closer to the opening.

"Fiona was everything to me," Ryan snarls at Seamus. "And ya killed her!"

"I did no such thing." Seamus speaks deliberately. "Ya're mad. Ya can't see straight."

"The answers right in front of you," I say, a realization hitting me. "Seamus would never kill anyone, and you're blind if you can't see who wouldn't think twice about taking a life."

A crease forms between his eyebrows. He's considering my implication, and I take the opportunity to continue.

"Nathair killed Fiona."

Ryan shakes his head. "No, they'd never do that to me."

A wave of sympathy washes over me as I watch Ryan's pain. Michael made the same mistake, and it cost him everything. "You know they would. Especially if they know you'd go after Seamus for it."

"Don't let them win," Seamus urges him. "Ya don't have to be like 'em. They didn't care about Fiona, and they don't care about ya, mate."

"Ya would think that, wouldn't ya?" He points the gun at

Seamus' chest, and I feel that whatever chance we had with Ryan has now passed.

I feel the urge to knock into Ryan and try to save Seamus, but this time, I control my emotions. I'm less than a foot from the opening now. Seamus shoots me a look, and I know this is my chance to escape. The boat sways on a large swell, and I use the distraction to dart from the room.

The sound of a gunshot echoes through the cabin, followed by a heavy thud.

I freeze at the stairs. *No. Please, God. Not Seamus.*

I give the stairs a last glance before running back down the corridor. As I come to the door, I collide with a body and hit the ground hard.

"Kayleigh!"

The sound of Seamus' voice sends relief spiraling through me. He helps me up, and I sway as another swell tosses the boat.

"What are ya doin'?"

"I heard the gunshot," I say through raspy breaths.

"It hit the wall. Gave me a chance to clock the ejjet." He closes the door and pushes a wooden table in front of it. "It's the best we can do right now. Come on. Let's get out of here." He takes my hand, and we hurry up the steps and onto the deck of the boat.

There's no sign of anyone. The boat swerves to the side, and Seamus grabs the wheel. "The tide is too strong for the autopilot. I need to take manual control."

I look at the sky above. The clouds are darkening, and there's an apprehension blowing in with the wind. The waves slap a warning against the sides of the boat.

"A storm's coming," I say, taking in the force of nature around us.

Seamus works with the navigation tool. "I have us headin' back to shore now. Let's just hope we make it in time."

"Do you think we will?" I hold my breath.

He looks to the sky. "I don't know."

The stairway door swings open, and Ryan climbs onto the deck. "This is where it all ends between you and me." There's blood streaming down his face from his nose, and he's unsteady on his feet.

With a burst of energy, he charges Seamus, knocking him to the floor.

"Seamus!" My scream is drowned out by the roar of thunder above.

The boat is thrown to the side, and I hold the sagging rope for balance. A wave of sea sickness turns my stomach before I steady myself.

"I don't want to fight ya!" Seamus screams over the roar of the wind. They've managed to stand even with the constant movement of the boat. A wave crashes onboard, and the cold water flows up to my waist as I cling to the rope.

As they round the deck, Ryan throws a punch that misses Seamus' head by mere inches. Seamus returns a swing that hits Ryan hard on the cheek. He stumbles back but regains his balances and returns with a fist to Seamus' nose. The boat rocks on a powerful swell, and Ryan releases a guttural sound as he leaps at Seamus, knocking them into the railing. A splintering sounds as Ryan falls through the rail. Seamus tries to grab him but loses his footing and falls to the deck, hitting his head on the metal rope tie. He lays unmoving as another wave floods the deck.

I need to save us.

I crawl over to him and pull him with renewed strength the short distance into the captain's galley. I close and lock the door and pray it keeps the water out. Large rain drops begin to splatter the windshield, blurring the path in front of us. I adjust the wheel gauge as I watched Seamus do many times and lock in the navigation. My knuckles whiten as I grip the wheel, squeezing hard to keep the boat balanced. The clouds converge, and a murky darkness settles over the sea. Every muscle in my body stiffens as the largest wave yet grows to a head only yards from the boat. The white of the crest tumbles forward and crashes onto the deck.

The boat rolls to the side, and I hold my breath as the water overcomes us.

CHAPTER FIFTEEN

I don't know how long we're under the water. Time seems to stand still. I remember the story Nora told us of Michael, James, and Erin on the water that day. James prayed for a way home, and the light came through. I close my eyes, the muffled deafness caused by the surrounding water even more profound without my sight.

Jesus my true knight, I pray to the One who can give me the strength I need. *Lead me home.*

The boat rolls, and I tumble against the cabin door. The water begins to subside, and I gasp for air. Seamus coughs, and I turn him over on his side. After expelling the water, his eyes blink open. He murmurs something before his eyes shut again.

"It's going to be okay," I tell him. "We're going home."

A glimmer of light shines through the windshield. This time I feel gratitude for the waves in front of us instead of fear. In the distance the rocky shore glimmers before us. I grab the wheel and drive into the next wave. Water splashes on the decks as we crest the wave. I have a newfound strength.

Nora, Malachy, Teagan, Finn, and Colonel are waiting for us as I direct the boat to dock. Colonel waves his tail desperately and barks as we near. An ambulance and the garda shout directions and are ready to assist. It takes a few tries, but I finally get close enough for them to tie the boat. The sun is now shining, and the wind has subsided, making it easier to steer into the lane. The broken rail and battered cabin are the only physical evidence of the storm. The EMTs rush onboard and strap Seamus on a long board. He groans and murmurs something, but I can't decipher what he says.

I kiss his forehead. "I love you, Seamus Murphy."

His eyes flicker. "I love ya, Kayleigh O'Reilly."

The EMTs carry him to the ambulance, and they drive off to the hospital.

A COUPLE OF WEEKS LATER, Seamus and I are sitting on the dock at the cottage. His head is still bandaged, but otherwise he made it out of the storm unharmed.

"The story ended up being so much more than I anticipated," I tell Seamus. "I hope Professor Gaffney sees an improvement in my writing. Although, either way, I know this time I wrote from the heart. Writing my story gave me so much more joy than any news article ever did."

"Don't think ya'll be a reporter after all?"

"No." I sigh. "I think my days of reporting are officially over."

"Ya're a good reporter, but I think yer heart may lie elsewhere. Perhaps in novels and helping others find their own stories?"

"The thought of focusing on my stories, writing here at

the cottage by the sea, it just feels right." There's a peace when you discover what you are meant to do. "Switching majors wasn't an easy decision, but I think creative writing is a much better fit than journalism ever was. But, I can't disregard journalism altogether though. The newspaper helped me discover myself again—a part of me I didn't even realize I was missing."

Journalism may not be in my future but something much better is. I've learned to write for fun again. To write what's on my heart and tell stories that, while not groundbreaking, are meaningful. And I get to help others discover their voice as well.

Seamus smiles at me, a full unreserved beam. "Now, don't ya ever lose her again. I'm a wee bit attached to her; ya know."

I laugh. "Well, I think she can say the same thing about you."

He wraps an arm around me, and I lean into him, laying my head on his muscular chest.

"I've learned that I don't want to just record other people's stories; I want to write my own. Professor Gaffney gave me the opportunity to explore the beginning of this, and I think it's time to see where my story leads"

Seamus kisses the top of my head. "I hope I'm in that story."

I turn my head up towards him. "Oh, you're there—right by my side."

"I think I'll like this story." He leans down and kisses me.

Colonel barks and climbs up on the bench between us, his large body pushing Seamus to the edge.

"Don't worry, you are too." I give his big nose a kiss.

Seamus grunts a response as he slides off the bench. "That beast is a menace."

I ruffle the fur on Colonel's head. "The best ones always are."

"I AM SO glad that course is over!" Samara tosses her notebook into the trash can.

I giggle. "It wasn't so bad."

She gives me a pointed look. "Don't go getting all sentimental on me. It was intense, and I think I need a few months to catch up on sleep—which I will be doing on the beach in about seventy-two hours. I need some relaxing days to get ready for next year."

I almost say I know what she means, but I stop myself because it's not true anymore. At one time I would have felt the same way, but the recent events have given me new goals and perspective. "Next year you're still onboard for helping with the writing program, right?"

Samara agreed to be a writing coach in the program. She is not only fun to work with but will easily connect with other writers.

"Absolutely. I wish there was a program like this for me in high school."

"Me too. But, at least we know we'll be helping others."

"And you get to do so with a certain handsome Irish guy." She nudges me with her shoulder.

I smile. "That Irish guy does bring a bit of charm."

Samara laughs. "I think it's time for him to introduce me to some of his friends."

"I'll talk to him." An image of Eion comes to mind. "Actually, how do you feel about Canada?"

"It's fine." She draws out the words. "Why?"

"Seamus has a friend who's a sports reporter in Canada.

His internship ends soon, and he'll be back in time for the Medieval Festival in Cloverdale this fall."

"Another reporter, huh?" She considers. "That could be interesting."

"I'll count you in for the festival then."

She laughs. "I could get used a knight in shining armor for once."

I think back to that day at the Medieval Festival. So much has changed since then. I was bitter and resentful. It was me against the world. Seamus helped my heart to heal. He showed me that no matter what happens, there's always a way for love to grow. Our love may not be a fairy tale or out of a Jane Austen novel, even as great as those are, but it will be real. Real knights help us to see the strength inside ourselves. And for that, I will be forever grateful.

We stop in front of the newspaper office.

Samara hugs me. "I'll see you when you get back."

"I'm looking forward to it. Don't work too hard this summer."

She holds up her hands. "I promise I will take a break."

I narrow my eyes at her. Samara takes a break as often as Teagan—which is to say, never. "Rest is being productive too. You don't want to get burned out before your career even begins."

"Come on, Kayleigh, you know the news doesn't rest. But," she says, opening the door to the office, "I promise to take a day or two. I have always wanted to see the Ring of Kerry."

I SIT across from Professor Gaffney in the library and wait as he reads the last of my story. He closes the portfolio and taps it against his knee.

"This is grand, Kayleigh," he says. "This is writin' from the heart."

"I'm so glad you think so." This story is different than any other story I've written. The words flowed from my heart in each experience and challenge I faced this year. It's the story of my own self-discovery.

He hands me the portfolio. "Ya already knew it though, didn't ya?"

I linger for a moment. "I've finally found a reason to write again, and that's made all of the difference."

"Is it safe to say that this story is part fiction and part biography?" His mouth quirks up on the side.

I grin back. "You could say that."

"Well, it sounds like ya've had an exciting year." He removes his glasses and cleans the lenses on his shirt sleeve. "I think with some editing and a couple of revisions, this will be a story people will love to read."

"I thought grades are due tomorrow. I don't think I could get any revisions in by then."

He puts his glasses back on and folds his hands in his lap. "I'm not talking about for the class. We can work out a publishing schedule that works for both of us."

I pause, unsure if I heard him correctly. "You want to publish my story?"

"Like I said, yer story is one people will love to read. And ya're a writer that I'd like to see continue to tell stories. But, if ya'd rather not publish—"

"No!" I say, a little too loudly. "It would be amazing. Thank you so much for this opportunity. It's just...I'm not sure this is where my story ends."

He hands my portfolio back to me. "I think ya may be right about that. By all means, let yer story take ya as far as it can. There's no rush. Write where yer heart leads ya. I'll be in touch."

As he walks away, I wonder where my heart will lead me.

CHAPTER SIXTEEN

It's our last Sunday before we leave to go back home to Maryland. I sit with Seamus, Cormac, Teagan, and Finn at the Kavanagh's supper table enjoying the spread of corned beef and cabbage. Just as we're finishing up, there's a knock at the door.

"Garda Connell, come in with ya," Nora says, waving her kitchen towel. "We have plenty left to go 'round."

"That's mighty kind, but I've already had supper." He places a hand over his stomach. "There's something I want to run by ye."

We all watch Garda Connell for any sign of what his news brings. He stands by the table and puts his hands in his pockets, looking like he's dreading whatever he's about the say.

"I've spoken with Caitlin. She's certain that Nathair is workin' out of Cloverdale. Our suspicions about someone in the community were on target. She doesn't know who it is, mind ya, so we best keep it to ourselves for the time bein'."

There's a murmur of disbelief from Malachy and Nora.

Garda Connell's lips form a thin line. "I'm also worried for

Caitlin. She's put herself in a place that is not only dangerous, but it's difficult to stay in touch with her without reinforcements.

"Then get her out," Malachy says, with a swift wave of his hand. "No need to be placin' her in harm's way."

Garda Connell looks down to the floor. "I tried, but she'll not be havin' it. She says she owes it to ye."

"That dear lass." Nora places her hand over her heart. "Is there anythin' we can do?"

"There's nothin' to be done right now. Caitlin says Nathair believes they have control over the town, so however they're connected, it's a strong link in the community." He looks to me. "I think it may be time to invite Maeve to Cloverdale. She may be our best ally."

"We'll talk with her." I take Seamus' hand. "I think she will want to help."

"I believe she will." Seamus gives my hand a squeeze. "No matter what happens with the board, we'll find a way."

"Nathair can't run this town without the board." Nora crosses her arms over her chest. "And not one soul on the board would risk Cloverdale for anything."

Garda Connell squares his jaw. "Nora, ya must believe by now that it's coming from within. The person may even be *on* the board."

"No, I won't believe it." Nora shakes her head.

"Nora is right that even if there's some bugger in town, there's still hope while the board is in place. The town is safe for now," Malachy says.

"If only there was a way to settle the feud peacefully," I say, remembering Michael and James.

"The Irish are a loyal people. The biggest hearts in the world, I'd wager. But, we can hold a grudge with the best of 'em." Malachy shakes his head.

"Right ya are," Nora agrees. "Big stubborn hearts."

Malachy and Nora's absolute belief that, in the end, all people are good, has touched my own heart. We are all flawed, but we were made good created for a beautiful purpose. The hard part is discovering what that purpose is and following God's path.

"How do we get through to those hearts?" I ask.

Everyone is quiet.

"Whatever we do, we can only do so much," Nora says. "The rest is up to them."

Malachy places a hand on Nora's shoulder. "We will stay loyal to our family and our town. We will stay strong and united."

<hr />

WE'RE ON A SISTERS' video call as I pack my bags the next day.

"I never thought journalism was right for you," Teagan says.

I think back to that day in Magnolia's Cafe. Jamie's eagerness for a story triumphed her sensitivity for the situation. "Sometimes the story can override everything else. I don't want that."

It wasn't long ago that I would have said Chris broke my heart. The memory of that day at the cafe is still vivid in my mind. But, there's not heartbreak over him that it evokes, but rather sadness for who I was then.

"After this year, I realize he didn't break my heart. He may have injured it and brought a coldness that I never want to have again. But, without that experience I wouldn't be where I am now. I have purpose now that I didn't before."

"It's crazy what a year in Ireland can do," Teagan says.

"So true. When I first came to Ireland, I wanted to go home. But that would have been the easy way out."

"That's true," Ashling says. "I mean, being kidnapped and steering a ship in the middle of a raging storm is the more adventurous way to go."

We laugh, and I can't wait for us all to be together again soon.

"Ashling has a point," Teagan says.

"She does," I agree. "We all need a little more adventure in our lives."

IT's my last evening in Ireland. The scent of seafood coddle wafts throughout the cottage. Seamus adds a handful of finely chopped parsley before stirring the soup with a large wooden spoon.

"It smells delicious." I scoot by him to retrieve the vintage table linens from the far cabinet. I pull out a small stack of blue linen napkins and two silver candle sticks, embossed with shamrocks growing up the sides. The pale yellow beeswax taper candles compliment the shade of the napkins.

I glance out the kitchen window at the foundation of the small stone building. Seamus is literally helping to build my dreams one log at a time. Seamus saved all of the money my parents gave him as rent for the cottage, and we're using it to get my *Cottage by the Sea Writing Retreat* up and running for the fall. Fiadh is already signed up as our first participant.

"I can't believe this is really happening."

Seamus follows my gaze. "There's still some money left, ya know. Maybe we could take a little retreat ourselves."

I turn to look at him. "What do you mean?"

"Well, Teagan and Finn went off to the Galapagos islands, and I was thinkin' we deserve some time away as well."

The idea of going away with Seamus fills me with excitement. "I like that idea. I hear Venice is nice this time of year."

"Venice, huh? I've always wanted to fish in the Adriatic Sea. I hear the sea bass is the stuff of legends."

"You know I love a good legend."

His grin spreads slowly as he cocks an eyebrow. "Are ya ready for an adventure, Kayleigh O'Reilly?"

The memory of those words from so long ago awakens my soul. I came to Ireland with lost and broken dreams, but this year brought about the biggest of changes in my life. Sometimes it's in the brokenness that you find the hope to start anew. It was the adventure I never expected, but the one that I needed the most.

I look into Seamus' eyes. "I'm ready."

EPILOGUE

"You're not stopping me now." Ashling shoots Seamus a warning glare as he reluctantly releases control of the steering wheel.

"Alright, now don't be turin' it too quickly or we'll all be goin' for a swim, ya hear?"

"Come on, Seamus." I take his hand and lead him to the back of the boat. "You taught her everything—"

"And repeated it about fifty times," Finn says.

I giggle. "She's been on this boat a million times. Sit with us and enjoy the ride."

"Bein' on a boat and steerin' a boat are two very different things." Seamus gives Ashling one last apprehensive glance before sliding onto the pin-striped seat cushion next to me.

"I thought cats hate the water?" He nods to the large gray and white cat sitting on the seat opposite us.

"O'Keeffe is a Maine coon," Teagan explains. "Most of them actually love the water. Their ancestors spent the majority of their lives on ships."

"It's true." I tell him. "Ashling doesn't go anywhere

without O'Keeffe. He loves the boat. You can consider him your first mate."

"Grand," Seamus says dryly.

I giggle at the exasperated look on his face. "Seamus, being on the lake is *peaceful*." I emphasize the last word. Berryville Lake is a quaint haven for our hometown during the summer. The sunlight sparkles off the water, giving our motorboat a heavenly glow.

"How fast can this thing go?" Seamus looks around at the nearby kayakers.

"Don't worry, Seamus," Teagan muses. "In Maryland, the maximum speed is six knots within one hundred feet of any shore, pier, bridge, or person. But, when we get into open water, we can pick up the speed a bit."

"How much is a bit?" He leans closer to me. "And why is the only one of us who has never driven a boat piloting us?"

"Ashling has never shown any interest in boating before, so we want her to try it," I explain.

"But, she's—"

"Yes, a bit unpredictable," I finish for him. "But, so is life. We just have to ride the waves."

I laugh at how I sound more and more like a writing teacher every day.

"You know, for someone who basically lives on the water, you should be enjoying this." Ashling sends him another annoyed look.

"How's Cody feel about you leaving for Ireland?" I ask her, trying to steer the conversation into safer waters.

"Oh, you know how it is. We're casual and all." She says this with a carefree roll of her eyes, but I can hear the note of disappointment in her voice. "He plans on backpacking across Europe, so our paths may cross again."

Unless God has other plans for you. I keep this thought to myself for now. "Well, we'll all be together again." I can't keep the giddiness out of my voice, imagining the three of us in Ireland together.

"It'll be grand," she says with an exaggerated Irish lilt.

The boat glides across the glistening water, and a spark of adventure lights in Ashling's eyes. In just a few weeks, the three of us will be together at Emerald Isle. After the past two years, and the adventures that Teagan and I had, I can only imagine what is in store for Ashling. She's always been the one to forge her own path. How will that match up with everything going on in Cloverdale?

Seamus kisses the top of my head. "The last time we were on the water together I was unconscious."

I run a finger over the scar by his left temple. "The water's a little calmer this time."

"'Tis." He wraps a protective arm around me as Ashling pushes the boat to a faster speed.

I long to be back in Ireland, even with the looming threat of Nathair. Things have been quiet in Cloverdale this summer, but we know something is on the horizon. I understand now what Teagan meant that day at the market—we can't live in fear. Not all battles are physical, like Seamus and Ryan in the boat. Some battles you can't see but are felt all the same. Nathair knows how to promote fear. And I refuse to give in by living my life in fear.

"Do you think it's the calm before the storm?" I ask Seamus.

He leans down and kisses me. "There's no storm we can't handle."

MEET THE AUTHOR

Colleen Marie writes sweet inspirational small-town romance with a sprinkle of humor, Irish luck, and southern charm. You can always count on stories full of beautiful country settings, quirky small towns, memorable characters, and clean, heartwarming romance. She earned her MFA in Creative Writing and is a member of the Catholic Writers Guild and American Christian Fiction Writers. A great love for animals and teaching led her to a career as a life scientist and science educator. Animals weave their way into her tales, bringing an added dose of humor (and undeniable adorableness) to the story.

Colleen Marie lives in a small town in Maryland with her husband, three children, and crew of lovable animals. When she's not writing, you can find her teaching biology at a local university, enjoying family hikes through the woods, or wrestling her adorable Australian shepherd puppy to keep him out of trouble—which is often a losing battle!

Visit her website at www.onespiritoflove.com and sign up for her monthly newsletter to learn about new releases, giveaways, and personal stories!

A LETTER FROM COLLEEN MARIE

Dear Readers,

The Emerald Isle University Series is a New Adult book series weaving the stories of three sisters and their adventures of self-discovery and love in Ireland—the land of rolling green hills, mysterious legends, and hidden treasures.

The idea for The Emerald Isle University Series began after experiencing Ireland for the first time. It is a land of dreams and treasures, and the Emerald Isle made a lasting impression on my heart.

As the years went by, I found myself immersed in the fields of life science and education while writing in those quiet moments. Then one day, I finally picked up the pencil and began outlining this trilogy. The series combines Irish culture and the beauty of the land with friendship, family, mystery, and second chance love.

I always hoped for a sister, so the idea of writing a series based on the connection between three sisters was a natural inclination. Each sister has her own unique story, but the bond of love and friendship between the three is unbreakable.

I hope you will join Teagan, Kayleigh, and Ashling on their adventures in the Emerald Isle, and remember, there's a treasure waiting for each of us—we just need to take a leap of faith!

If you enjoyed Kayleigh's story, please take a moment to leave a review on Goodreads, Amazon, and other retailers. Your reviews are greatly appreciated and help to share The Emerald Isle University Series with others.

Follow along on social media!
Instagram @colleenmarieauthor, One Spirit of Love
Facebook Colleen Marie - Author, One Spirit of Love
X Colleen Marie - Author, @One Spirit of Love
Pinterest Colleen Marie - Author @colleenmarieauthor, One Spirit of Love

OTHER BOOKS BY COLLEEN MARIE

TEAGAN'S TREASURE
Emerald Isle University Series Book #1

Teagan O'Reilly has one goal upon graduation—to be accepted into Emerald Isle University's Science Research Internship and spend the summer in Ireland competing for a spot in the university's coveted research program. When her acceptance letter finally arrives, Teagan is more determined than ever to win a spot into the program. She's prepared for everything until she learns her partner is none other than Finn Connolly, her first love and the boy who broke her heart.

Past feelings reignite as Teagan and Finn travel to Brigid's Crossing in the small town of Cloverdale, Ireland, to begin their internship. Their research project quickly comes to life on the Kavanagh's horse farm, bringing new life to the farm and Teagan's dreams.

Teagan soon discovers that the farm is in financial trouble, jeopardizing her meticulously planned research, and it needs a miracle to be saved. The rolling hills of the Irish countryside are hiding a secret, and the answer may lie in the legendary tale of the missing Kildare Emerald. When a plot to steal the emerald from the Kavanagh's land is uncovered, the safety of the farm and their chance at the research position lies in the balance.

As time begins to run out, Teagan is torn between winning the research position and helping the Kavanaghs save the farm. Teagan is forced to decide where her heart lies, but will her choice make her lose everything she's always dreamed of, or will she gain more than she ever imagined?

NEXT BOOK IN THE SERIES

Ashling's Anchor
Emerald Isle University Series Book #3
Coming 2026

Ashling O'Reilly has the heart of an artist. When she receives a scholarship for the Emerald Isle University's legendary Fine Arts program, she travels to Ireland in hopes of bringing her artistic dreams to life. As she joins her sisters, Teagan and Kayleigh, at the university and settles into life on the Kavanagh's horse farm, she begins to question whether she truly belongs there.

Feeling lost and confused, she accepts an invitation to backpack through Europe with her free-spirited ex-boyfriend. But just as she's about the leave Ireland, her eyes are opened to the traditional art of metal work by the quiet and brooding farrier, Cormac Byrne. Ashling takes a leap of faith and joins Cormac in a dual apprenticeship with the town's blacksmith. Her dreams are stoked by the fire, and her heart warms to the idea of love for the first time. As she finds purpose in her artistic calling, she's thrust into the midst of a decades-old Irish feud threatening to destroy the town and the people she loves.

Ashling becomes entangled in a web of ancient folklore, lies, and deception. With the town on the brink of destruction, she races to uncover who's behind the vengeful attack before it's too late. Ashling must decide how far she will go to save the town and traditions that have found a place in her heart. As the town begins to crumble, will Ashling find the strength to fight for what she believes in?

ACKNOWLEDGMENTS

I want to start, as always, by thanking you, the reader, for joining Kayleigh on her journey. I hope you enjoyed your time in Cloverdale, Ireland. I invite you to sign-up for my newsletter to learn about upcoming releases, giveaways, and events. I hope you will return for Ashling's story, the third book in the Emerald Isle University series.

Wishing heartfelt thanks to:

Vinspire Publishing for believing in the O'Reilly sister's and giving the Emerald Isle University series it's first home.

All of my early readers. Your feedback, reviews, and testimonials mean so much.

My editor, Allison Ramirez of Trinity Tree Publishing, for your brilliant way of encouraging me while bringing out the best of the story. Thank you for everything and I look forward to working together on Ashling's story.

My family and friends for your unceasing support and love.

My parents for your constant love, fun adventures, and wonderful memories, especially those on the water.

Connor, Brody, and Emma for inspiring me every day. My love for you is deeper than the depths of the sea.

My husband, Bill. Thank you for your continual support of my dreams and being by my side every step of the way. I love you!

And above all else, to Jesus, to whom this book is dedicated. You're my Knight and Your love radiates from my every word.

AUTHOR'S NOTE

Have you ever had a teacher who inspired you to follow your dreams? In middle school, my English teacher asked me to stay behind after class one day. After the other students left the classroom, we sat down, and she told me how she believed I had a gift for writing. It was because of her encouragement that I began writing in earnest. I created story binders of characters and filled many notebooks with the stories that filled my mind.

A similar experience with my high school English teacher gave my writing new life. I published a few poems in various anthologies and wrote stories in the quiet hours of the morning in our school chapel. At our senior honors assembly, I was surprised to learn that I had won the Maryland's Catholic Daughter's of America Poetry contest. I had no idea that my poem was selected from the school, nor that it was in the running for the state contest. I went up on the stage and accepted my award and small scholarship. As I walked down the stairs to return to my seat, I met the encouraging eyes of my English teacher, who always believed in me.

About fifteen years later, while teaching at my alma mater,

my high school English teacher passed away. The impact she had on my writing and the memory of her encouraging words led to a time of discernment in my life. I felt called to write again, and a few months later I was accepted into an MFA program for creative writing, and my professional career came to life.

In *Kayleigh's Knight*, Kayleigh finds the inspiration she needs to write from the heart and creates the *Cottage by the Sea Writing Retreat* as a way to help other writers find their purpose. Kayleigh's story shows the impact an encouraging teacher or friend can have. Always speak words of encouragement to others. You never know how much your words can change someone's life.

Today I write under the title of One Spirit of Love. I founded my animal-assisted learning and wellness program, Spirit of Love, in 2018, and it was founded on faith, love, and small-town community—the same foundation of my writing. As I reflected on my writing, it occurred to me that every aspect of my life has one thing in common, one reality that is at the center of it all—the One Spirit.

Jesus put the dream of writing in my heart, and it grows every day with His love.

www.OneSpiritofLove.com

www.ingramcontent.com/pod-product-compliance
Lightning Source LLC
Chambersburg PA
CBHW020032310726
48970CB00007B/2217